The Baby Grand, The Moon in July, & Me

The Baby Grand, The Moon in July, & Me

Joyce Annette Barnes

Dial Books for Young Readers  NEW YORK

Published by Dial Books for Young Readers
A Division of Penguin Books USA Inc.
375 Hudson Street • New York, New York 10014
Copyright © 1994 by Joyce Annette Barnes
All rights reserved • Designed by Kris Waldherr
Printed in the U.S.A.
First Edition
1 3 5 7 9 10 8 6 4 2

Library of Congress Cataloging in Publication Data
Barnes, Joyce Annette.
The baby grand, the moon in July, and me/ by Joyce Annette Barnes.
p. cm.
Summary: In 1969, the launching of the *Apollo 11* moon rocket fuels
ten-year-old Annie's dream of becoming an astronaut, but problems at home make
her realize that it will take hard work to make her dream come true.
ISBN 0-8037-1586-2 (trade).—ISBN 0-8037-1600-1 (library)
[1. Astronautics—Fiction. 2. Afro-Americans—Fiction. 3. Family
life—Fiction.] I. Title.
PZ7.B2624Bab 1994 [Fic]—dc20 93-17984 CIP AC

Special thanks to Kyle Herring of the Johnson Space Flight Center
in Houston, Texas, and Dick Young of the Kennedy Space Flight Center
in Florida for their help in verifying the *Apollo 11* flight transcripts.

For my mother, for Justin, for Pilar

Wednesday, July 16, 1969

LAUNCH DAY

Chapter One

I'm half awake and still dreaming when I hear:

"This is Apollo-Saturn launch control. T minus 61 minutes and counting—T minus 61 minutes on the Apollo 11 countdown, and all elements are 'go' at this time. Astronaut Neil Armstrong has just completed a series of checks on that big service propulsion system engine that—"

"Annie!"

My eyes fly open. I've been jerked back to Earth from the far reaches of the universe by my mother's voice.

"Look at you." Mama leans over and clicks off the TV set, then turns and fixes me with a look. "You slept all night in front of that TV again, didn't you? Honestly, you're gonna start glowing one day."

My mother's given to exaggeration, especially when she's scolding me. It is true that I left the TV on and perched on the living room sofa last night so I'd be here, and awake, for the lift-off this morning. I must have fallen asleep. Still, I remember hearing "The Star-Spangled Banner" playing, so I was awake when the station signed off at 12:30 A.M. Therefore, *all night* is simply incorrect.

But there's no time to explain all of this. "Did I miss it?" I reach for the television knob. But, even though she's only five feet two, Mama blocks me like a linebacker.

"Oh, no," she says, pointing. "Upstairs."

"But I don't want to miss this! Please, just let me turn the TV back on. Please, please, pleeeaase!"

Her eyes narrow. Mama hates to hear me whine, so this usually works. "Miss what, Annie?" she snaps.

I smack my forehead and roll my eyes to heaven. It's incredible to me that I have to remind her again. *"Apollo 11*, Mama. To the moon. We're taking off for the moon."

Mama looks at the TV set, then looks back at me as if she doesn't believe a word I've said. "Mama, this is *the* most exciting thing happening in the whole

4

world today. Please don't make me miss it. Please, please, pleeaase—"

She waves me silent and, reluctantly, clicks the set back on, giving me another doubtful look. We both watch as the screen goes from black to snowy and then clears. The newsman with the puffy eyes and the monotone voice is saying, "We are still 'go' with *Apollo 11*. It's T minus 60 minutes to the lift-off. That's one hour from now."

"Whew." I wipe my forehead and aim a big grin straight at my mother. "They haven't launched it yet." I want her to know she has not absolutely ruined my day. But already she's lost interest in that whole matter and has spotted something else to get on my case about. In a second she's at my hair smoothing and tucking in the two braids going down the sides of my head.

"Look at you," Mama groans. "You look like you've been to the moon and back yourself." (See, exaggeration.) "Run upstairs and get the comb and brush offa my dresser. Just because your mother works, you don't have to look like an orphan child."

"*Mama* . . ."

"Go." She points me to the stairs.

Further whining is useless and just might land me in more trouble. I change my tone and walk purposefully up a few steps. "I don't know why you can't stay home and watch it with me. I mean, going to the moon is enough reason to miss a day of work. Heckie! It should be a national holiday."

"Well, it's not," Mama says. "If the President doesn't think it's enough of a holiday, who are we to say? I have to go to work today just like any other day."

She watches me climb some more steps.

"Besides, I got too much to worry about right here at 154 Oakridge Avenue to care about some men on the moon. Now go on up and do like I said, you hear me?"

"No, I do," I mumble.

"And stop that crazy talk!" She keeps watching until I'm about halfway up and then pivots on her heels and strides off toward the kitchen. "Oh, and Annie, tell your daddy coffee'll be ready in a few minutes. Tell him to hurry now. I'd like to be on time for work at least once a week. Today's just as good a day as any. Men on the moon. What next?" And she disappears beyond the kitchen door.

I run the rest of the way up the stairs, call "Daddymamasaidcoffee'sready," grab up the brush (forget the comb), and race back downstairs, jumping over the last four steps. In less than fifteen seconds I'm in front of the TV again.

They're showing a wide shot of the *Saturn V* rocket, which looks taller than fifty church steeples and whiter than brand-new snow. Red letters spell U-S-A down its side. An American flag is painted above the letters, on the side of the rocket. The cone-shaped command module is where the crew will live for the next eight days. The command module has windows so that the astronauts can look back from thousands and thousands of miles away and still see Earth.

Attached to the top of the command module, the silver escape tower points into the sky, like a needle ready to give space a shot in the arm.

The rocket, straight and tall against the sky, reminds me of a soldier decked out in full dress uniform, standing at attention. It kinda takes your breath away.

After a while I hear Daddy humming at the top of the stairs. He takes his time getting ready, unlike Mama who's always rushing. And even though he's six feet tall and over 200 pounds (well over), he sounds light as a dancer coming down the steps. His friends call him Slim. I guess he was once.

"Hey, Shoopaloop!" Daddy calls when he spots me.

"Hi, Daddy. You gonna watch the lift-off with me?" I'm still trying to get somebody else in this house interested in this momentous event.

"Can't, Shoop. Gotta go see The Man about a paycheck." He goes straight for the front door to get the newspaper, "which just oughta be sitting there waiting for me, much as I pay for it," he always says. As usual, it's not. The paper boy takes his time with his deliveries. I think he stays home and watches the morning cartoons first. It's a good thing we don't get the evening paper, or we might not get it until midnight. Anyway, as soon as Daddy opens the door, the paper comes flying in and just misses his head.

Daddy ducks, then runs outside, his big size not slowing him down one bit. "Little punk!" he yells, waving his fist. I cover my mouth to keep from laughing, but it comes out anyway. Some of the neighborhood boys are afraid of my father because of his size and his big voice. But that newspaper boy just waves and pedals his rickety bike on down the street.

I can't stop giggling, even when Daddy comes back in grumbling under his breath. "What's so funny?"

"You!"

He squares his shoulders and tries to look insulted. But before long his face crinkles into a smile, the dimples going deep into his cheeks.

"Wanna do the dance?" he says, bending his arms up in a pose.

"Yeah!" I lift my arms up too and we both scoot across the floor, gyrating like his favorite comedian, Jackie Gleason. *"Yat tat, yat tat, yatta ta! Yatta ta, yatta ta, yatta!"* he sings, dancing toward his chair.

He does some smooth turns and glides down into it. "How sweet it is!"

Once he gets settled, Daddy pulls his reading glasses from the front pocket of his work uniform, unfolds the paper, and peers at the front page. Of course, most of the news is about the space mission. "Rockets to the moon, huh?" He pulls at his beardless chin. "Hmmmmmm."

I'm standing over his chair, breathing down his neck, trying to read.

"You interested in this stuff, Annie?"

"You know it!" I hover closer.

"Think you might want to read all about it?"

"Yes, sir!" I say. He knows I'm itching to grab the paper. Still, he takes his good little time reading, keeping his eyes fixed someplace on the page much longer than it takes him to read it. I'm shifting on my feet, anxious for him to turn to where the stories continue inside. But instead, he refolds the paper and holds it in front of him, out of my reach.

"Okay," Daddy announces, "spell some words for me and it's yours."

"No problem," I say.

"Okay, my little spelling-bee champ."

"I was just runner-up," I correct him.

Daddy grins. "That's champ enough for me."

I get into my spelling-bee posture. Feet solid,

hands folded before me, eyes steady, deep breath.

"You ready?"

"Yep."

"Okay." He leans over and reopens the paper, scanning the front page. "Spell *lunar module.*"

"That's too easy. Lunar module. L-U-N-A-R M-O-D-U-L-E. Lunar module."

He nods. "Now, spell *velocity.*"

I spell that too. All the words he gives me out of the newspaper are easy like that, I tell him. So, he politely hands me the paper just as Mama comes back in.

"Slim, coffee's ready." Her announcement to Daddy is followed by a stern look at me. "Annie didn't I tell you to get the brush *and* comb?"

I glance at the brush where I've casually thrown it on the table. Mama picks it up and waves it at me, giving me this long-suffering look.

"I'm sorry, Mama," I say, and I truly am. "It's just that we're taking off for the moon today. Who can think about hair?"

Mama's not buying those apples. She scoots me up the stairs. "If you think I'm leaving here with your head looking like a chicken coop, you're wrong. It's not enough I gotta go out of here for eight hours, Annie. But I have to go behind you *constantly* and redo everything you do. Just once, Annie, just once

I'd like to see somebody make the effort the first time. Just once!"

She says all of this with one breath. My mother has the strongest lungs. She has a beautiful singing voice too. You wouldn't necessarily know it right now, though.

Daddy stands up during Mama's tirade and goes over to turn on his hi-fi player. As I reach the top steps I hear him say, "Do what your mother says, Annie. So she can just shut up."

I feel bad about upsetting Mama. And she's right. I really don't listen very well, or follow through when told to do something. I have to work on that, I say to myself for the umpteenth time.

On the way back down I hear my parents talking in the dining room. Daddy has his favorite record playing, a jazz album. I don't know the name of the man playing the piano, but I know the song, "Take Five." I've heard it ever since I've been alive, it seems. And I kinda like it. The sound is "mellow," Daddy always says. "It grooves." To me it sounds like a rocking chair feels. The music floating up the dark stairway like that makes it seem more like evening than morning.

Even from here I can smell the strong coffee they're drinking. Every now and then I hear the newspaper shifting, so I know Daddy's reading. Mama's voice is soft. I scoot down a couple of steps and settle there. Might as well let them enjoy their moments together, I decide, twirling the comb in my hand.

"She's the smart one," I hear Daddy say.

"She sure is."

"Sharp as a tack."

"They both are."

"*Sshpt!*" Daddy says. It's a sound he makes when he's disgusted.

Mama's voice rises. "Matthew's smart too."

"He's a bum."

"Now, Slim. He's very talented."

"Okay, Sara. He's a talented bum." I stifle a giggle. Mama's right. My brother *is* talented. He's never had one piano lesson, yet he can play any song from the radio after only hearing it once. I wonder why Daddy doesn't know this.

"He's not a bum, Slim. He works hard at that store."

Daddy huffs. "Selling pianos? Ain't nobody around here can even afford to buy a piano. What kinda job is that, Sara?"

"It's an honest job. Besides, what he really wants is to play—"

"Jazz!" Daddy almost shouts. "Look, Sara, I'm a jazz lover, but I know ain't no money in that. *Sshpt!*"

Jazz musicians the ones borrowing money from lowly, uneducated mechanics like me."

Daddy works at the air force base about thirty miles out of town. He fixes airplanes, which *I* think is an important job, but Daddy seems to dislike it. Or maybe it's just that he doesn't like having to work two jobs. He drives a taxicab some nights until midnight. Mama is a secretary, and she likes her job.

"I hope you ain't hitching your star to that one, 'cause you in for a big disappointment."

"He's gonna be famous one day, according to him. A big celebrity." Mama's voice has a teasing quality to it, like she only half believes that. Daddy just grumbles, not wanting to grace that statement with a reply. "Well, the point is," Mama goes on, still with a giggle in her voice, "we've got two bright and talented children, either one of whom could get rich and take us outta here."

"The girl, maybe. But not that boy. He's a lazy bum. If he had any sense, he'd a signed up to serve his country in this here war. There's boys dying over there in Vietnam, and all he can think about is playing music."

"Slim," Mama says. "Don't start." I'm glad she cut him off. I don't like to think of Matty going to the war. Daddy sometimes tells me stories about his being in "The Big One," meaning World War II. I've

13

seen pictures of him in army fatigues, a heavy rifle strapped across his shoulder. He looks young and proud, and I guess for him, being in the war was a good experience. But Matty doesn't feel that way at all. He said he'd rather run off to Canada and play jazz.

They are silent again for a few moments. Even though the music is still playing, suddenly the house seems quiet too. Matty's asleep, and I'm in suspended animation. Then the newspaper crinkles again.

"They got stereo equipment on sale down at High's Electronics," Daddy says.

Mama doesn't answer.

"Says they'll finance it for twenty-four months."

"Oh, no, Slim Armstrong," Mama suddenly pipes in. "Not another thing on credit."

"Aw, Sara."

"First it was the car. Then the deep freezer. Now a stereo? At this rate I'll be working till I'm sixty-five."

"That's the normal age for retirement, Sara."

"Yes, but I'm only supposed to be working temporarily, remember. Till we get the bills down," Mama huffs. "Six years. Some temporary."

The newspaper crunches together. Daddy's chair

scrapes loudly against the wooden floor. "Forget it. Forget the stereo!" he shouts.

Mama's cup slams into its saucer. Her chair scrapes the floor too. "Forget the stereo? Forget that?" Her voice is squeaky tight, high-pitched like it gets when she's really upset. "Forget my life, Slim. Okay? Forget everything I ever wanted in this poor world. Forget nice furniture and a big house. Forget a co-ordinated kitchen with appliances that look like they belong in the same era. Forget working away from home and having a daughter who practically has to raise herself!"

Mama's exaggerating again. No way do I get to raise myself. When Matty's not around to boss me, Mama takes me to my grandparents' house. Or, she hires my cousin Lindy to "baby-sit." Lindy's a teen-ager who spends most of her time watching the soap operas and baby-sitting the telephone. Still, she manages to follow Mama's orders to a *T*.

But this is not the time to bring that up. Instead, I run down the rest of the steps, trying to make a lot of noise. "Here's the comb, Mama," I say, out of breath.

Mama looks at me and seems to calm down about twenty notches in a matter of seconds. For a long time we just stand there saying nothing. Daddy is looking at Mama, and she and I are looking at each other. Then, with her mouth tight, she says, "It's too late now, Annie." She scoops up the empty cups and goes back to the kitchen.

The music has stopped. After a while I go back upstairs to wash, dress, and comb my hair myself. I take my time and keep repeating: *My mother and father do not hate each other. I am a good daughter. Matty is a good son. There's a war someplace far away, but Matty's not going. And today, we're blasting off for the moon.*

Chapter Two

"Make sure you eat breakfast, Annie. Before you go outside. And brush your teeth afterward. And after lunch." Mama fusses at me the whole time she walks to the car. "And no sugar sandwiches, you hear me, Annie?"

"Yes, I don't," I reply, grinning.

"Yeah, well your teeth are gonna all fall out," Mama calls back. Another hyperbolic statement.

By the time I take up position front and center before the TV, there's only ten minutes left until lift-off. I have a glass of milk in one hand and the newspaper in the other. One article says that each day on the moon equals about 14 earth days and that the moon's only one-fourth the size of the earth. It can get as hot as 250 degrees Fahrenheit above and as cold as 250 degrees Fahrenheit below zero. It weighs about 81 billion billion tons. Of course, I know all of this already.

On an inside page is a picture of the full moon glowing in a velvet-black sky. I scribble zeroes in the margins, trying to figure out how to write 81 billion billion. Then, here comes Matty tumbling down the stairs at full speed, blasting his transistor radio.

"Whassis sisappenin'!" he says, his standard greeting, which makes no sense.

"Turn it down!" I yell.

Matty turns his music even louder and sings all out of tune, dancing across the floor, up on the sofa, shaking his head at me. He lets "I Need Money" play all the way through at a volume to blow your ears away.

"I can't hear!"

When the song ends, Matty finally clicks off his radio. "Aw, Annie, you don't need to be watching that stuff anyway. Capitalist propaganda is all it is."

"Proper *what?*"

"It's all a fiction. A Hollywood production. And you're a fool to believe it." He wags his finger in my face.

I slap it away, outraged. "No, it isn't. And no, I'm not!"

"—Besides, it ain't got nothing to do with us."

"Does too," I insist. "One of the astronauts even has our last name. Neil Armstrong. And he's the commander!"

This stops him, but he just looks at me, rolls his eyes, and winds his finger around his head like I'm lost in space. "Annie," Matty says, "if stupidity was a drop of water, you'd be the Pacific Ocean."

"Well, if ugliness was one teeny, tiny grain of sand, you'd be the Sahara Desert."

Which isn't true. Matty is handsome. He's the color of toast and is tall with a perfectly shaped afro that makes him look even taller. Girls call here all the time, asking for "Sterling," which is his middle name. Nobody around here calls him that. "Sterling's for excellence," he explains when I tease him about it.

"No time for childish games today, Annie—"

"You're only nine years older than me."

"—'Cause after today, I'ma set off my own rockets."

Now it's my turn to roll my eyes. Matty is always spouting off about something he's gonna do or be. I half listen to his bragging, which he says is "no brag, just fact." I don't even ask him what he's talking about. I turn my attention back to the *real* rocket.

"It's not childish," I grumble. "It's all very important, especially to someone like me—a lunarian."

19

(I got that word from my science teacher last year. He was a lunarian and was so excited about the upcoming mission to the moon, he convinced me I should be one too.)

Matty sucks his teeth at me. "A lunatic," he sneers and then just stares out of the window.

On TV another voice takes over, and this one is excited. "Eighty-second mark has now been passed. We'll go on full internal power at the 50-second mark in the countdown. Guidance system goes on internal at 17 seconds, leading up to the ignition sequence at 8.9 seconds. We're approaching the 60-second mark on the *Apollo 11* mission. T minus 60 seconds and counting."

"Matty, it's about to lift off!"

"Who cares, Annie." He keeps staring out the window.

"Watch it with me, pleeeaase!" But it's no use. I'm riveted to the set, but he's pacing behind me like a nervous cat, paying me no mind. "You're gonna miss it." My voices shakes.

"We have just passed the 50-second mark. Our transfer is complete on an internal power with the launch vehicle at this time. Forty seconds away from the *Apollo 11* lift-off. All the second stage tanks now pressurized. Thirty-five seconds and counting. . . ."

All of a sudden, Matty yells, "It's here!" and tears out of the house.

"Matty," I scream, chasing behind him to the door. He's already halfway down the walk. I can't believe he's deserted me at this moment, but I can't bother with him right now. Whatever he's talking about can't be as exciting as going to the moon.

"We are still 'go' with *Apollo 11*. . . . Twenty seconds and counting."

I go back to the TV.

"T minus 15 seconds, guidance is internal. 12–11–10–9—. Ignition sequence starts . . ."

For each count, my heart beats twenty times.

"6–5–4—"

I can hardly breathe.

"2–1, zero! All engines running! Lift-off! We have a lift-off, thirty-two minutes past the hour. Lift-off on *Apollo 11*."

It looks like an explosion. Orange hot flames pour from the five booster engines and smoke spreads across the launchpad in thick waves. But the rocket doesn't move. And I can't breathe. What if it won't go up? What if the whole things burns up in a blaze as the millions and millions of gallons of fuel just ignite and flames rise all the way up to the escape tower?

I'm thinking all of this, and holding my breath, in the seconds it takes for the steel arms that hold the rocket to the Earth to fall back like tall buildings in a Godzilla movie. And then, just as easy as you please, just like somebody's reached down and lifted it up with their hands, the rocket starts to rise. Slowly, at first, and straight up. Then getting faster and lighter and farther and farther away. The sound is like hundreds of jet airplanes taking off at once. "The building is shaking," the newsman says.

Apollo 11 climbs higher and higher into the sky, the fiery white tail like a fan, trailing blue, orange, and lightning-white fire, then white, and finally brown smoke across the sky.

"Matty," I squeak, hardly able to say a word. I stand there and watch until the rocket becomes a silver pinpoint in the sky. Then I run outside, getting my voice on the way.

"Matty!" I yell. "Can you see it? Can we see *Apollo 11* from here?"

Outside, the sun is so bright I have to scroonch my eyes practically closed. The sky is blue and clear. Of course, I know you can't see the spacecraft from here, but I stare up into the sky anyway.

The creak of a heavy metal door opening pulls my attention back to ground level. A moving truck is parked in front of our house. Two men in dingy white T-shirts climb into the back of the truck while Matty hops around from one side to the other saying, "Be careful, man. Be careful." The men ignore him.

Even though I'm mad at Matty for not watching the launch with me, I have to go investigate. Matty calls me nosy, but I know I'm just curious. "What's that?" I say, trying to sound nonchalant.

"It's a piano, Annie. A baby grand piano."

"It is?" I run to the truck, losing all pretenses, and peek into the back to get a good look. At first, all I see in the darkness of the truck are the bodies of the two men and something covered over by a dull green quilt. Then, when I look down, I see these four jet-black wood-carved legs on golden wheels.

"A piano! Why didn't anybody tell me? I get left out of all the important decisions. A piano! A baby grand piano!"

Not that those words mean much to me. What's a baby piano? Is there an adult piano? The only pianos I've ever seen—the ones at school, the uprights at church, and the nicest one, the one Miss James, my piano teacher, has in her living room—don't have any other name but "piano." What kind of piano is a "baby grand"?

Grunting and heaving and, I think, cussing, the two men roll the piano to a point where it can come down a rickety ramp. The wheels clang across the rippled surface of the ramp, and with each bump, Matty winces. I cover my ears against the racket until the men get the piano on level ground. Once it is sitting on the sidewalk in front of our yard, the men straighten themselves up and lean against their truck.

"You roll it on up there, son," the older man says to the other, stopping to wipe his sweaty face with a handkerchief.

"Why me?"

" 'Cause I say so," the first replies. They look at each other and grin, looking like they plan to leave the piano right there on the sidewalk.

"Hey, what's up, man?" Matty says, but not like he usually says it when he's talking to his friends. "You gonna finish the job, or what?"

"Hold onto your pants, boy. We's having a coffee break."

The two men laugh, and I notice they both have moustaches. Red ones. They favor each other in other ways too. I glance over at the side of the truck and read: Rybicki and Son, Movers.

"I don't see no coffee," Matty says to Mr. Rybicki, Sr., talking like he's forgetting his manners. "So why don't you go on and finish the job like you're supposed to. I'm paying you for this, after all."

With a surprised look Mr. Rybicki stands straight

and comes posing in Matty's face. I see my brother's jaw tighten and quiver, which makes my own heart race.

Mr. Rybicki, Sr., is not a tall man, not as tall as Matty, but he looks muscled, even more so than his son. His face is pink under the red hair left on his head. He squints at Matty like he's looking into a bright light. "I say we's on a break. You got anything more to say about it, we'll leave the piano right here."

He and Matty stand there like tigers ready to fight. The three of them seem to have moved a distance away from me, or me from them. Maybe it's the hot sun beating down on my head, or maybe I was staring too long up into the sky. Or it could be that I'm too wrapped up in this spaceflight business, I don't know. But I feel suddenly far away. Like I've lifted off, floated over the others. Weightless. Invisible, but still able to hear and see them. They are like a TV show I'm watching from the moon.

"Matty," I say, but he can't hear me. He and Mr. Rybicki stare each other down. They don't even seem to be breathing. I try to warn Matty again, but my voice is 250,000 miles away and no one on Earth can hear me.

Then, to my relief, my brother steps back and lets out a long breath. Still, he keeps staring right back at Mr. Rybicki. "People in this community call on you a lot to move their things. Mr. Shaw relies on you too. But there're other movers. Maybe I'll just let Shaw know the quality of service you give—in his name."

Mr. Rybicki's eyes blink real fast. His son steps up between the two of them. "Pop," he says, "come on."

The son turns to Matty and asks, "Where do you want this?"

Matty doesn't speak, but he jerks his head toward our garage in the backyard. The two movers start to roll the piano up the driveway. Mr. Rybicki, Sr., mumbles something about "disrespect."

Matty does not follow right away, but he never takes his eyes off of them. I float back down to Earth. "You see, Annie," he says to me. "You see why I don't care about no NASA space program or any of that?"

He stomps away toward the garage.

Actually, I don't see.

Chapter Three

I watch the three of them disappear behind the house. I really would like to get a look at that piano, but I don't follow them. Instead, I go sit on my front porch and wait for the Tippets to come outside. I don't have to wait long.

The first one out is Dodie Tippet. I suppress a groan. She slams their screen door shut and calls, "Annie!" waving idiotically. Dodie runs down their front steps and across the street without even checking for cars. "What you all got, Annie?" she asks, pointing to the truck.

"Don't you know how to look before you cross the street?"

Dodie hunches up her shoulders and grins, her

small, even teeth showing. To my relief Sue comes out next. Unlike Dodie, though, Sue takes her own sweet time coming over. She checks the street out up and down, not so much to look for cars, but to see if anyone's watching her. Then, she switches across like somebody *is*. Sue's what you might call "fast."

Dodie keeps pestering me about the truck. I ignore her till Sue joins us.

"It's a piano," I say calmly, like we get pianos delivered to our house every Wednesday.

Dodie's voice shoots up an octave. *"Oowee,* can I play it? I can play piano, can't I, Sue."

"Shut uuup!" Sue replies, pained.

"Make me!" Dodie's favorite words.

Sue switches her hip to her younger sister and gives me a look. Sue and I are both going on eleven. We think Dodie, at eight, is hyperactive even for her age and wish their mother'd put her on medication. "It's Matty's piano," I tell Dodie. "He bought it." I know Matty won't let her within a ten-mile range of that piano, but I keep that to myself.

Sue blows a bubble and pops it. "Well, what's he gonna do with it?" she asks in a smart-alecky way.

"Play it, I suppose. Gretchen Susanne." Sue hates to be called by her full name. She rolls her eyes at me. "Annette Funicello," she shoots back. Which is not my name. It's Annie Armstrong, no middle name, and Sue knows that. I stick my tongue out back at her. Believe it or not, Sue and I are best friends. She's just got this crazy streak that'll drive you nuts. In fact, I think all the Tippet children are a little touched, all except Claude.

Claude is two years older than Sue and me, but he acts so much better even than their older brother, Heath. Heath is mean and thinks because he's fourteen, he can boss us. Claude, however, is nice and smart and, well, cute. Claude and I both want to be NASA astronauts when we grow up, so lately we've been reading and talking about space and time and how one day we want to travel at light speed. In fact, I'm beginning to spend more time with Claude than I do with Sue, which is making her even crazier than normal.

Sue will say things to me like, "Claude is so annoying, always got some big idea he wants to do."

And I'll reply, innocently, "That's not annoying. I like Claude's big ideas." Then Sue and Dodie will promptly break out with, "Annie's got a boyfriend, tisky tisky tadio! How do you know? Tisky tisky tadio! She told me so! That's how I know-oh!"

"I do not," I insist, but they always keep it up.

As if my thoughts are a summons, here comes Claude out of the door. He waves and then waits while Heath and Cheron, the Tippets' youngest sister, settle some dispute on the porch. Cheron's only four and a half but so smart we usually don't mind her hanging around us. As a matter of fact, Cheron usually bosses us around.

Heath, Cheron, and Claude cross the street toward my house. "Just be quiet," I warn Sue and Dodie. Sue smirks and Dodie giggles, but they're not singing for once. The three of us meet them at the curb, and as if by a signal, we all turn and head down the block and across the street to the little Oakwood community park that we call The Jungle.

The Jungle used to be an asphalt lot, but one year some city workers came and made it a park. It's not much. It has no grass, just gravel and sand that our mothers hate us to track into the house. The playthings are all weather-beaten wood, except for the slide and some painted animal-bouncing toys that even Cheron won't play on. Still, this is our official meeting place, which we've turned into a country club, a palace, a battlefield, a sports arena, and a boardroom. Right now, it's just our playground.

Claude leans his back against the jungle gym, next to me. "Did you see it, Annie? All that smoke?"

"Like an explosion. It was kinda scary," I admit.

Claude stands up. "Aw, I wasn't scared. I knew it would be all right."

"So did I," I say, defensively. "I mean, I understood why all the engines were firing, to boost the rocket away from Earth's gravitational force."

"Aw, Annie," Heath cuts me off. "What do you know about it?"

"More than you do, Heath. I know those engines were carrying over six million pounds of fuel." I start spouting off other numbers which I'm not sure are exactly accurate. "And the rocket can go up to 25,000 miles per hour. I even know how much fuel it burns *per second*. What do you know, Heath Tippet?"

Claude, Sue, Dodie, and Cheron say, "Ooooo." But Heath just waves his hand at me. "It's all a fiction, anyway." Heath's the kind of guy who adores telling little kids that there's no Santa Claus.

Claude stops me from grabbing his brother's neck. "He's just mad, Annie, 'cause he got put back." We all laugh, and now Heath tries to go for Claude's neck. He grabs his shirt instead and gives Claude's head a smack. We all say, "Oooooo!" The next thing I know, those two are duking it out, kicking up sand and getting it all up under our socks.

"I'm just telling her the truth," Heath manages to say while he ducks Claude's punches. "Ain't no need in Annie going on about all that astronaut stuff. You think you gonna be an astronaut?" he says to me. "Whoever heard of a girl astronaut."

"I won't be a girl then," I say. "I'll be a woman."

"Don't listen to him, Annie," Claude puts in.

"She'd better listen. Ain't no women astronauts either. You watched that lift-off today, Annie. You didn't see one woman at all. All you saw were rows and rows and rows of men. Look in all those space books you got, Annie. Ever see any women astronauts in them?"

"S-so." My voice falters. Heath nods, but just then Claude smacks his head.

Heath just laughs. "You want to get anywhere near the moon, Annie, you better marry an astronaut."

I can't answer him, I'm so mad. Heath does this to me all the time. He finds any reason to contradict what I say and to challenge any idea I have.

I don't even want to strangle him any longer. It's gone way beyond that. I want him off this Earth.

Why do I let those Tippets make me crazy?

Claude, seeing me, turns red. "Hey, shut up!" he yells. He charges at Heath and knocks him down. They roll around in the sand some more, getting filthy. We just stand and watch them, shaking our heads.

"I'ma tell," Dodie keeps saying.

"Boys," Sue complains.

Cheron, who has been quiet during the whole melee, suddenly yells, "Stop!" We're all so shocked to hear this big voice coming from her little body that we do stop. "This is ra-dicalus," she declares and places her pudgy brown hands on her nonexistent hips. We fall down laughing. We can't help it. She's so cute with her brownie-like face, and the fat braids that sprout out all over her head. She gives us all a stern look.

Claude is the first to recover. "Okay, Princess C. We'll stop." He gets up and brushes the sand out of his hair.

Cheron nods and settles back on the ground. She doesn't mind being called Princess because she believes she is one. "Let's not talk about astronauts anymore," she commands.

"Anyway," Dodie says, "you know the weather's gonna turn bad with all those rockets in out-of-space."

"It's outer space, you moron. There is no out-of-space," Claude says. I keep quiet, figuring it's best to ignore comments like Dodie's.

"It's true," she insists. "Those rockets make the clouds change and the weather turn ugly."

"Shut up, Dodie," Sue says.

"Make me!"

Sue lets out a big, impatient, totally-fed-up-with-Dodie breath.

"Fine," I say, realizing that Claude and I will have to continue our discussion later. "Then, what're we gonna do?"

Dodie pipes up. "I know! Let's play tetherball." Of course, she would suggest that, being the best girl player around. We don't have a real tetherball or even a tetherball pole. We just take any old ball, tie it up in a sling, tie a rope to it, and hang this from the stop sign. We've bent a few stop sign poles this way.

"Naw," Cheron says, "that'll bring too many people over here. I don't *feel like* all those people."

It's amazing how much we let this little tyke boss us around. I have to cover my face to keep from laughing again, which I know will upset her. Cheron likes to be taken seriously.

She scrambles to her feet and dusts sand from her flowered shorts. "Let's go—see the Humpbacked Man," she announces. "I wanna see him! And the Horsefaced Lady too. Are they married to each other?"

"No, Cheron. The Horsefaced Lady lives on the east side of town. This is the west side. Only the Humpbacked Man lives here," Heath explains.

"The Horsefaced Lady's mother laughed at a horse when she was pregnant with her," Heath continues.

"Ooowee," Dodie puts in. "You said 'preg—'!"

Heath ignores her. "She lives with her mother 'cause only her mother could love her." Heath finds this funny. "The Humpbacked Man's got this disease, and if he touches you, you'll get Humpbacked

34

Man's disease and have to walk like this." He demonstrates for us, exaggerating a stooped pose and a craggy face.

None of us has ever actually seen this Humpbacked Man, but we all know where he lives. His house is down our block, around the corner, and across two more streets. The street is a steep hill with only one house on it, the Humpbacked Man's house. His place is where Oakwood ends.

The house sits way back from the street on top of a hilly yard with a carved wrought-iron fence all around it. There is no sign that says "Keep Out" attached to the gate, but there might as well be. As far as we know, no one has ever been brave enough to go into his yard.

Claude says, "If you wanna see him, Princess C, I'll take you."

Dodie starts to protest. "Naw, no way. I ain't going over there." Sue and I look at each other. Truth is, going to see the Humpbacked Man is more appealing if Dodie's staying home. With a quick exchange of glances we all get up from our places and start out of the park.

"I'ma tell. I'ma tell Mama," Dodie says. "You know she said we better not go over there. I'ma tell!"

"Shut up, Eggs." Claude calls her Eggs for Eggs Benedict because Dodie's always running back and telling things, like Benedict Arnold.

"Make me!" Dodie screams. We leave her, gratefully, and head down the street toward the Humpbacked Man's house.

We stop at Mr. Hershey's store on the corner of the next block. It's a small white building, part store, part house. Mr. and Mrs. Hershey live above. We all peer into the window at the assortment of plastic toys and wrapped candies there, saying, "That's mine. No, that's mine."

Sue ogles a row of birthstone rings, lined up by month. "I'ma get one for each of my fingers," she claims.

Heath looks at the price of them. "Fifty cents each! I remember when they were a quarter." His eyes slide off and his lips move as he multiplies. *"Whoowee.* Where you gonna get five dollars for some rings, huh?"

"Don't you worry about that," Sue says. She flings her head away and proceeds down the steps, confident, no doubt, that some boy she knows will buy each and every ring she wants. We all shrug at each other and continue on.

Claude walks beside me, walking on his tiptoes and bowed legs like he does. It makes him look like a cowboy who's been riding a horse for too long. He keeps looking at me sideways and looking away when I look back. "What's up, Claude?" I say. The others, hearing me, start teasing him. "What's up, Claude? What's up, Claude?" It sounds like "Clod." I'm sorry I started it. Claude just ignores them.

"D'you like those rings, Annie?" Claude says shyly as we walk together.

I hunch my shoulders. "Yeah, they're pretty."

He keeps silent for some more steps. Then, out of the blue, he asks me, "Well, *would* you marry an astronaut? I mean, uh, if you couldn't be one?"

I don't answer him for a while. I'm trying to remain calm. After a few moments I simply say, "I'm gonna *be* one," and run to catch up with the others.

Before long we reach the Humpbacked Man's street.

"You think he's home," Cheron asks, her voice now a whisper.

Heath goes into his know-it-all stance. "Of course he's home. And he probably knows we're here. He can smell children, and he's got superpower hearing. He knows we're here, and he's just waiting in there for us to enter through that iron gate, into his trap. Then, he'll catch us, and we'll all grow these basketball-sized humps on our backs and walk like this—" He slouches over. Cheron begins to whimper.

"What'd you do that for?" Claude yells at Heath.

"Well, she wanted to come!"

Sue and I try to quiet the little girl, and Claude finally picks her up. He presses her fat brown cheek against his sand-colored one. Cheron's his favorite, and vice versa. "You still wanna see him, Princess C?" Cheron nods. "Then you have to be brave." She nods again, and he puts her down.

With new resolve we all climb up to the base of the fence and crouch down. We peep over the scraggly row of bushes along the fence and see the house with its peeling white paint and dull green roof. The windows are all shut up, even in this summer heat. All the curtains are drawn. The yard is weedy and turning brown, no flowers anywhere, no birdbaths, nothing that looks like it's living.

The place looks like a fit house for some monstrous human like a humpbacked man. It's not like Mrs. Rosen's, the witch's, house, which looks just like any other house. The only way we know she's a witch is because one day a dead man was found on her porch, and no one knew who he was, or where he'd come from, or how he'd died.

"He needs his grass cut," Claude observes.

"How we gonna get him to come out?" Sue asks.

We look at each other a minute. "Well"—I finally say what we're all thinking—"somebody's gotta go up there and knock on the door."

Heath immediately says, "Not me. I have to carry Cheron in case he chases us. I run faster than anybody else." Which is true.

"You go, Claude," Heath says.

"Why me?" Claude says and I want to say at the same time, "Why him?"

"Well, I'm not going," Sue declares, looking at her nails as if somehow the Humpbacked Man might break one.

"Don't even look at me," Cheron puts in, not that anybody was.

I hesitate. Then Claude says, "I'll do it."

I frown. "Maybe this isn't such a good idea. Maybe Dodie was right." They all look at me like I've just said the moon's made of cheese. Claude raises his eyebrows at me, then stands straight up, his head above the hedges.

"I'm not scared," he says. "Y'all slip through the gate and scoot on up closer. See? To those bushes right in front of the porch. I'll run up there, knock on the door, and run back down to you. Then, when he comes to the door, we all jump up, look, and run away. It's simple." Claude grins at us as he strides confidently to the gate and opens it. We scuttle behind him and take up our position behind the shrubs.

"Just watch me," Claude says as he climbs up the steps and approaches the closed front door, "and maybe you'll learn something."

We do watch him. Heath covers his mouth to keep from laughing. What he thinks is funny only Heath knows. Sue is silent and just stares. Cheron and I are holding our breath as Claude risks his neck (and back) for us. I feel like shouting to him, "Claude, come back. It's too dangerous!" But there's something exciting about it too, and part of me wishes I were the brave one going up those steps, up to the door, to confront the unknown.

Claude is still grinning as he glances back at us. He's at the top of the steps, still turned to face us, walking backward, when all of a sudden the screen door slams back against the wooden house. The clack makes us all jump, and Claude just freezes. "Whosat downere!" a voice cackles. Claude's grin drops like a stage-one booster.

Cheron, bless her little heart, screams, "The Humpbacked Man!" and takes off across the yard. Heath goes after her, yelling her name, and screaming back at us to run. He didn't have to. Sue and I are a half second behind him. "Run, Claude!" I manage to choke out.

We all pick up speed going down the hill, and we

let the momentum carry us all the way across the street and halfway down the next block before we stop. In a second, after we know we're a safe distance away and no awful, monstrous creature is stalking us, we laugh, bent over, with relief. But it only takes another second for me to notice the missing person.

"Where's Claude!"

"I thought he was right behind you."

"I never saw him leave the porch!"

Cheron wails. Heath groans.

Sue picks up Cheron. "Hush, hush." But there's no comforting her. People are starting to peep out of their windows at us.

Heath starts back up the block. "Stay here," he instructs us. "I'll go back—"

"No!" we all cry in a chorus and grab him to keep him from going. One brother in the clutches of the Humpbacked Man is enough. Poor Claude. Poor cute, sweet, brave Claude—now a victim, no doubt, of that dread disease. I want to wail like Cheron, but I know that won't help anything. Heath looks at the three of us holding on to him and throws up his hands.

Just as Heath wrestles out of our grip, Claude appears across the street, his hands jammed in his pockets, his legs loose and bowed, grinning. "Fraidy cats!" he calls.

We run up to meet him, bubbling over with questions, and give him a hero's welcome, complete with tears (Cheron's) and pats on the back. "Y'all like to scared that old white man to death," Claude laughs, throwing his head back.

"He's white?" I say.

"As the day is long." Claude grins. This is a real discovery. No white people live in our neighborhood. Or at least, that's what we thought.

Cheron gasps. "Is he humpbacked for real?"

"Yep. And guess what else?" Claude pauses dramatically. "I'ma cut his lawn Friday morning. For five dollars!"

He struts past us, his head pointing skyward. We fall in beside him, and even Heath has to give him grudging respect. "Y'all oughta be shamed of yourselves, being afraid of that old man," Claude goes on. "He's just an old man."

"Well, we didn't know," I say in our defense. But even as I say it, I know it's no excuse. What kinda astronaut am I gonna make, I think miserably, if I'm too afraid to go up and knock on an old man's door?

Claude brags all the way home. Why not? He deserves to. Still, when he comes up beside me and whispers, "You shoulda seen him, Annie," I can't think of anything to say, so I roll my eyes at him and stalk right into the house.

Chapter Four

With the excitement of the morning, I've almost forgotten about Matty and his baby grand piano. Until I hear him out in the garage, plinking out notes and playing chords, and doing those riffs up the treble keys. I make myself a sugar sandwich and walk out the back door of the house.

Our garage sits at the end of the yard. Next to it are two peach trees, my daddy's prized possessions. Before these, there is a stretch of green, evenly cut and trimmed grass, bordered by a skinny iron fence. Daddy has built a stone patio, complete with a stone barbecue grill and a rock garden for my mother. Behind the garage is the alley that separates our house from the one on the next block.

It's dark when I step into the garage from the door in front because Matty has the large doors that open out into the alley closed. But I can see that he's swept the floor clean and cleared away all the other gunk that collects in garages. He's wiped the windows and piled knickknacks to one side. The garage looks neat. "It's dark in here," I say, flicking on the light.

Matty, standing next to the baby grand piano with a white cloth in his hand, acts like he doesn't hear me. He reaches out and wipes a spot. The piano is already glistening.

"Oooh," I coo, "it's pretty."

"It's *more* than pretty, Annie."

When the boy is right, the boy is right. Even in the weak light I can see it is as black as a starless midnight. Still, the surface shines. It stands on four black legs that end in golden wheels. Gold writing spells "Kawai" right above middle *C,* and at one end of the cover there's a queer golden sign that looks like a half-moon drawn in a squiggly hand. I cross over to get a closer look. "What's that?"

"Step back!" Matty shouts, stopping me in my tracks. "Don't you dare touch it with your sugary hands." He gives me a hard look. "That's their mark of excellence," he says, and then slowly lifts the piano top and props it open on a stick. More gold. And silver. The piano takes on a look of royalty.

I finish my sandwich and clean my hands on my top. Meanwhile, Matty has wiped the cloth over the whole thing again. "Now can I play it?"

He thinks a long moment. "Just wait, Annie. Be cool now." He inches me closer, careful that I don't make any sudden moves. "This," he preaches, "ain't no ordinary piano, 'cause I ain't no ordinary piano player. Let me tell you a few things about a grand piano."

He points inside. "See these. Bass strings, strung diagonally over the sound board at just the right tension." He touches a key. "Listen. Perfect pitch. Me and this piano belong together."

"I hear it," I say, impatient.

"Annie, you don't even know what you're listening for." He sits down on the bench. "Now, listen." He starts playing. I want to remind him that I'm the one who wanted to play, but I keep quiet. He plays a few chords and does some more fancy finger work up the treble keys, then folds his hands and looks at me. "You gotta have the proper appreciation for an instrument like this." He goes on and on, and I try to look interested. But all I want to do is play it!

"It's not like I'll never let you play it, Annie. But what you have to understand is that this piano is for serious artists. Like me. Not people like you who just play because somebody makes you. If Mama didn't

45

want you to play the piano so bad, you'd never even look at one."

"Yes, I would," I insist, but I know there's some truth in what he says. I like piano music. I just don't like the hours of my life I have to spend practicing. I'd rather be out playing, or reading, or making up stories myself. But I know how much my mother loves to hear me play, how proud she is to sit and listen to me. She's always going on about her aunt Bettye she had when she was little. "She used to give performances in her parlor. That's what we called the living room then. Oh, it was beautiful music. Brahms, Chopin. She could play them all." Mama's face would be all dreamy saying this, then she'd get this regretful look. "I wanted to play, but there was no time for it. Always something else to get done. Washing, cooking, cotton to pick."

"Mama, were you a slave?" I'd asked, amazed. She laughed and said, "No, Annie. Of course not!"

Anyway, whenever she gets like this, she reminds me how much music can lift her spirits. How it was all worth it to have two children who could play piano, even if she couldn't. Truth is, I'm nowhere near as good as Matty, but I try, for her.

"If you're gonna be great at something, Annie, you gotta want it really bad. More than that. I don't play just because I want to," Matty says. "I play 'cause I have to. It's part of me. You understand what I'm saying?"

I don't actually, but then I hardly ever understand my big brother. But I do know how much he loves to play. He doesn't have to say a word for me to know that. You can see it. You can hear it.

So, when he launches into one of his jazz pieces, I know he's not gonna stop playing for a while. "This is one I wrote myself, Annie. It's called 'The Living Is Easy.' "

I pull out one of the lawn chairs and unfold it fully, stretch out on it in the garage, and just listen.

"Wake up, lazy bones." Matty kicks the chair.

It's late afternoon. I can tell by the way the light is coming in through the windows. Matty stands over me, his hand out. I take his hand and he pulls me up. My neck is stiff.

"What time is it?"

"Four-thirty. Time for you to wash up for dinner."

I groan, grumble, and complain like I do every day around this time. Mama insists that every day I take a bath and put on fresh clothes before she gets home from work. She says that after a day of playing hard, I'll feel much better if I'm clean and fresh for dinner. The trouble comes in trying to stay fresh and clean until dinner is ready.

With that ritual behind me I go back out to the garage. "Now can I play?" I croak. He looks at me, knowing he can't avoid this much longer. So, he lets me sit down, and then he sits next to me on the bench. Without having to say a word, we both start playing, me on the bass notes, Matty on the treble. It's a song he taught me a year ago, when he used to walk me to the church so I could practice. This was when I was just starting lessons, and I had these simple minuets to play, and songs like "Onward Christian Soldiers." Matty would sit with me for a while, and we'd play "Peter Gunn," a rocking song with trills and riffs. One day, Reverend Leander heard us and sent Matty out. He told our mother, and she wouldn't let Matty go with me anymore. We play "Peter Gunn" and some other tunes we know. Then the garage door creaks open.

"Mama," Matty says, startled. His voice makes me jump.

Mama stands at the door, not saying a word at first. She still has on her dress and heels from work. Matty and I are silent too. She looks across at us and at the piano like she can't believe what she's seeing. Finally, in one breath, she exclaims, "What in the world is this?"

I blurt out, "It's a piano!"

"I can see that, Annie."

48

"A baby grand piano. Matty bought it." Matty shoots me a look.

Mama takes a few steps forward, as if she's unsure she can walk. She treats the piano like it's a dangerous animal. "What's she talking about, Matthew? What have you done?"

"You got a big mouth," Matty tells me.

"But," I protest, confused, "you did buy it!"

"No, he didn't, Annie. He's playing a joke on you. Tell her, Matthew. Tell her it's a joke. Tell me!"

Matty sighs and stands up before the piano like he's protecting it. "I bought it. It's mine."

I thought Mama would be all too happy to see this beautiful piano. I was wrong. She pops off like a package of firecrackers.

"What do you mean? You don't have money for no piano!" Her voice is high-pitched and tight.

"I had to," Matty puts in.

"Had to? This ain't no girl, Matthew."

"Mr. Shaw sold it to me because he knows how much work I put into it. He taught me how to tune it, and I helped refinish the case. Look at this." Mama won't look at the piano, just keeps staring at Matty. "He gave me a twenty-percent discount on it. And I can pay it over the next thirty-six mon—"

"Oh, no!" Mama falls back like she's gonna faint. Matty and I rush to catch her, but she waves us away.

49

She steadies herself against the wall. "No. Not on credit. Tell me you didn't."

Matty will not look at her now. He sets his face and watches the floor. Mama, waiting for him to say something, hardens by the second. Finally, she takes a deep breath. "It's going back."

"No!" Matty shouts.

"No!" I say, in unison.

"Yes!" Mama screams. "We can't afford this."

"I'll get another job," Matty puts in. "Two jobs."

"You could get three jobs and we still couldn't afford it. These are hard times, Matt. We need our money for other things."

Matty throws his hands into the air. "Things? Like what? College? You the only one wants me to go to college." His voice is rising. He stares at Mama and she stares back at him, looking at him like he's a crazy man. He calms down a little, jams his hands into his pockets. Then, it's like Mama just remembers I'm there. She spies me beside the piano.

"Annie, go into the house. I'll be there in a minute. I want to talk to Matt."

"Yes, ma'am," I say. Mama pats my shoulder as I walk past. I try to smile. "Please let us keep it," I say. "Please, please, pleeaase!"

"Inside, girl."

I glance quickly at both of them as I go out. I close

the door and go directly inside, not wanting to eaves-
drop on this conversation.

Before I can settle into a chair in front of the TV,
Mama and Matty have brought their discussion inside. Now they are shouting.

Mama goes straight for the telephone. Matty is two
seconds behind her, protesting all the way.

"Any money you make, you ought to help out
around here. Look at this place, Matthew. This furniture's as old as you are. We had it when you were
born. And how about food? You eat like it's going out
of style tomorrow. It's about time you started being
more responsible and stopped throwing money at the
moon!"

It's strange to me that she would say that, when
she seemed so uninterested in the moon earlier.

Matty watches as she dials. "Now you sound like
Daddy."

Her hand falters, but she keeps going. They glare
at each other. I've never seen Matty so disrespectful
before. I want to punch that smart-alecky look off his
face—but then again, I also want the piano to stay.

"Hello, Shaw's Music Store?" Mama says into the
phone.

"Mama, if you do this—"

She cups her hand over the telephone. "Don't
threaten me, boy. You may be a musician, but I'm

51

your mother." Back on the phone. "Yes, this is Mrs. Armstrong. Matthew's mother. Is Mr. Shaw in?"

"Mama, please," Matty says, trying another tactic.

I keep quiet, looking from one to another. Matty's face looks like it's melting, and Mama's looks as hard as stone.

"He's not? Well, please have him call me as soon as he returns." Mama gives someone our number and hangs up. "It's going back, Matthew," she says again.

"You can't do this. It's mine."

Mama ignores this, goes into the kitchen. Matty follows her and I follow him.

"That's my dream out there," he continues.

That stops her. She turns to face him, both of us, since I'm standing next to my big brother. She looks like she doesn't want to say something, but she has to.

She gives us this terrible, sad look. "Poor folks ain't got no business with dreams. Not expensive ones like a baby grand piano. Look, if I could, if I was rich, some society lady with old money, don't you think I'd buy you a piano? And Annie one too. I'd buy all kinds of classy, sophisticated items—oil paintings to hang on our walls, expensive vases from China to put fresh flowers in. Custom draperies. A luxury car for your daddy like he's always wanted. So he can ride to his two jobs in style—"

She breaks off. For a minute her face softens, and she looks so pretty. The slanting sun through the kitchen window catches in her eyes and warms her golden complexion. The frown lines fall from her forehead. For a few moments; then they're back.

"But, I ain't rich, am I. I'm a working woman. I'm sorry." She turns abruptly and starts to run water.

Matty and I say nothing. I sink into a nearby chair. Eventually, he walks out the back door. Before he closes it, he turns to me.

"If you're as smart as they say you are, Annie, you'll get outta here as fast as you can. Fast. Before they try to take the fuel outta your rockets too."

A few minutes later we hear him on the piano. He's playing that song he wrote. It doesn't sound easy at all. The sound is muted, but we can tell he's pounding. Mama starts to peel carrots and potatoes, and I'm tracing a pattern in the plastic placemats on our table. We both are quiet, just listening to Matty's furious piano playing.

Chapter Five

"Well, tell me about the lift-off."

Mama and I are eating dinner at the kitchen table. She's made a chicken and vegetable potpie with a cornbread crust. Matty's still playing the baby grand.

"It was great. First, there was this pure white smoke—just billowing all along the launch pad, thick as whipped cream, you know? Then, you saw this white and orange fire, brighter than the sun, shoot out underneath. And the rocket just lifts up—" I raise my pointed hand from the launchpad table. "Then, after a while it disappeared."

Mama takes a sip of coffee. She hasn't even tasted her potpie. "That's remarkable, Annie."

"One day, I'm going to the moon."

She looks surprised. "You are?"

"Yep. They say one day there'll be regular trips back and forth to the moon. Shuttle flights, just like you catch a bus to go downtown."

"Surely not." Mama looks at me like I've just come alive before her eyes. "Annie, would you wanta ride on one of those things?"

"Ride on it?" I screw up my face. "Heckie, I wanta *fly* it!"

Mama laughs. "Oh, Annie." She looks at me and shakes her head. "You think that's really what you want to do?"

"I know it. Can you just imagine—seeing outer space. Looking back out of the shuttle window and seeing the Earth turning, with nothing to hold it up but the laws of nature." Mama watches me silently, looking at me and, I think, listening to Matty at the same time. I take another forkful of food and make a point of chewing thirty times, mouth closed.

Mama's face is calm, but alert, like she's hearing and thinking a thousand things all at once. "Say that again, Annie," she says suddenly.

I give her a quizzical look. "Say 'I know it' again," she says.

"I know it?" I say. Then, when she smiles, I repeat it, with more conviction. "I know it!"

"Oh, gosh." Mama stands up, her shoulders going

up with a big sigh and coming down again heavily. Matty's no longer pounding the keys, but he's been playing continuously since he stormed out of the house. Now, he's playing that song again, "The Living Is Easy." This time, it sounds soft, mellow. It's like one of those jazz songs that Daddy would say "grooves."

"I just love that," Mama says.

After dinner I beg her to let me practice my lessons on the baby grand. But she doesn't want me to touch it, saying, "It's not ours."

"Neither is the church piano. And this one is so much better. You should play it, Mama. The keys don't stick. It's like you hardly have to press 'em."

"We shouldn't get attached."

"But I hate using that old rickety piano at church. It's out of tune. And it smells moldy."

Mama frowns. She's drying the dinner dishes, but when I say this, she puts the towel down and turns to me. I shut up quick. Mama looks upset for a moment, but then her face changes.

"Look, Annie. You're being ungrateful. Reverend Leander's nice enough to come open the church for you every other evening and let you practice. He doesn't have to do that. And besides . . . besides . . ." She doesn't finish.

I shift my tone. "Mama," I begin tentatively,

"Matty needs a break. He needs to eat. He's been playing a long time."

This stops her. She regards me again. "He told me I could practice on it. Maybe if I remind him, he'll come in and eat."

"Oh, gosh," Mama says, then, "go ahead."

"Yippee!" I'm up in a flash of a wink and out the door with my composition books and sheet music before she can change her mind.

"Tell Matt to come on in here," she calls after me.

"Okay. Okay, okay, okay!"

"Mama says it's time to eat."

Matty stops abruptly and swings around on the piano bench, his long legs straddling it. He looks wild-eyed, like he doesn't even see me. His shoes are off, of course, because that's how he plays.

"Earth to Matty."

"Yeah?"

"Mama said you have to let me practice." So I stretched it a bit. "And she said you should come have dinner." I hold my breath, for I know he's gonna refuse.

But, surprise of surprises, he doesn't. "Yeah, sure." He hops up from the bench and puts his shoes on. "Go on, Annie. Play. And don't get up till I come back."

"Wowee!" I exclaim and clamber over to the baby grand. He's almost out the door before I can sit down, and something about the way he's leaving makes me suspicious. "Where're you going?"

"Don't worry. Just play."

"But Mama said—"

"No time for eating. I got things to do." He gives me a wink and is gone.

Oh, boy. Is he weird.

I play through my easy pieces like "Off We Go!" and then do my scales. Mama comes out there with me after a while. "Where's Matt?"

"Dunno. He said I could play till he comes back."

She walks to the piano, still acting like it'll bite her. Gingerly she sits down beside me and finally gets up enough courage to hit a note. Middle *C*. The sound seems to startle her. "Oh!" she says.

"Wanna play a duet?" I offer. My mother and I have worked on one of the duets from my primary composition book, a simple minuet.

She smiles like she's embarrassed and puts her hands lightly on the white keys. Quickly she removes them and folds them in her lap. "Oh, I can't play."

I start my part anyway. Eventually, I know, she'll join in. Soon she does, drawn by the simple sweet sound of the music. We play it through twice before she gets up abruptly and steps away.

"Go on. Practice your recital piece."

I had been avoiding that piece, but slowly I pull the sheet music for the "Barcarolle" from beneath the other books.

"It's too hard," I complain, looking at the pages exploding with notes.

"Practice," she says, giving me a nod. So I start in and play it through several times. Mama claps after each one, even though in my opinion I sound worse each time. I stumble over parts, miss the fingering, lose count, and commit all other kinds of piano music murder. Finally, I do get through it one time without any major mess-ups.

"You're so good at this, Annie. You and Matt."

"He's better."

"He loves it more," she says after a pause. With that, she steps back again—not from fear this time, but like she wants to get another look at us—me and the baby grand. In the early evening sunlight it gleams black and magnificent. I watch her for a moment, then turn and start playing the "Barcarolle" again. For Mama, 'cause it eases her mind so.

Too soon, Matty bursts back in.

"Whassis sisappenin'!" he shouts. He spots Mama sitting there. "Hey, Mom!"

He no longer looks angry or even strange. He

whisks past us and goes to open the large back doors of the garage. The sun pours into half of the garage, making the other part seem even darker. A van is pulled up in the alley. Inside is Matty's friend Oscar Gallon. He hops out of the driver's seat and waves his big hands at us.

"Hi, Mrs. Armstrong. Hey, Birdlegs!" He calls me that because I'm so skinny. He steps around to the back of the van and opens it, and then I notice another person in the passenger seat. Eddie Sands slips out on his side and nods, mumbling a hello to us. Eddie is thin and coconut brown, with wavy black hair that he's had "processed." He doesn't talk much.

"Hi, Gal," Mama says, a little puzzled. "Hello, Eddie."

Matty starts unloading things from the van and bringing them into the garage. A black instrument case, a silver drum stand. "Matty?" Mama says.

He pretends he's too preoccupied to hear her, but when she moves to block him, he has to respond. "Oh, we're having a jam session tonight. You know. Gal's got his drums and Sands has his guitar and amp. I got the piano, so—"

"Matthew!"

"Get up, Annie," Matty barks. I ignore him, watching the three of them maneuver around Mama to set up the instruments.

"Hey, Birdlegs," Gallon calls to me. "Give us a hand here."

"My name's not Birdlegs." But I'm only too glad to help. A jam session!

"Matthew," Mama says again. "You know—" Matty carefully places the stand for the cymbals on the floor. Then he gently pulls Mama out of the line of traffic and to the front garage door.

"I know, Mama. I just want to do this. One night. That's all I'm asking."

"I don't want you thinking it's yours," Mama insists.

Matty grins. "I already think that." Just then we hear the telephone ring from inside the house. I'd almost forgotten that the piano had to go back, that Mama'd left a message for Mr. Shaw at the music store. She gives Matty a look that he interprets as consent, for he claps his hands and leaps back out to the van. Mama quickly turns and goes inside.

"All right, let's jam! Annie! Annie! We're gonna party tonight. Hey, hey, hey!"

Matty picks me up and swings me around. Then Gal gives me noogies on my head. The mood in the garage has definitely picked up. Even the quiet Eddie has to laugh.

Once everything's in place and the wires are connected, they each go solemnly to their instruments.

Matty lets me sit next to him. The garage doors are all open, and Matty's kicked off his shoes. Eddie twangs his guitar a few times, pulls out some smooth chords. Then he makes the amp screech, and we all hold our ears. Gallon goes *tadat boom* on his drums. Matty just sits there.

"That's a nice piece of work," Eddie says, nodding toward the piano. Matty nods back.

"What d'ya say, cats? Where do we start?"

Gallon rubs his hands together and tosses his sticks into the air. "How about some Cannonball Adderly?"

"Mercy, mercy, me," Matty says. He puts his hands on the keyboard and counts. "One, two, one-two-three-four. . . ." And the jam session is under way.

Chapter Six

By nightfall the garage truly is jammed. So is the alley. So is the yard. People are up in the branches of the peach trees, groovin'. People from blocks away, people I don't know, have gathered around our yard to hear the music that's pouring from our garage.

They play Cannonball Adderly, Nat Adderly, Ramsey Lewis, and Donald Byrd. Then they start taking requests and people holler "Green Onions!" and "Movin' on Up!"

People sing along, all out of tune, but nobody cares. Snapping fingers, swaying heads, closed eyes, tapping toes. Bodies bump up against one another. People break out into dances like the "Tighten Up" and the

"Camel Walk." And when the band starts to play "Say It Loud!" it's like a riot erupts around our yard.

Some people say we got a lot of manners,
Some say it's a lot of nerve.
I say we don't quit moving, till we get
What we deserve.
Say it loud!
"I'm black and I'm proud!"

People shout, raising their fists.

It goes on for hours. More people come. Nobody leaves. Mama at some point goes inside and makes gallons of iced tea, which she doles out in paper cups. Then she goes back around with a trash bag to collect the empty ones. Later she sits with a group of neighbor ladies who have a special section on one side of the garage. She laughs so much I think her sides must hurt. And every once in a while these ladies put in a special request for church songs they want to hear. Mama asks for her favorite, "Motherless Child."

The place gets a little quieter as Matty starts it off. At first, the music sounds nothing like the song we all know because Matty is improvising. Then, after a few minutes of Matty's solo, we hear the familiar strains of the song, coming slowly and softly from his piano, and Niecy, the soprano soloist from the church choir, starts to sing. It's enough to bring tears to your eyes.

I see the Tippets (all but Cheron) squeeze through the crowd. I wave at them, and we all go out to the backyard.

"This is so cool," Heath says. It takes a lot for Heath to admit that something outside of his own doing is cool. I slap a five with him. This is a night for everybody to get along. Even Dodie is tolerable. Before long we have our own party, dancing on the patio. Sue is the most hip about the new dances.

"Do the 'Four Corners,' " she shouts, like she's calling for a square dance. And when we look at her like she's lost her mind, she demonstrates for us. "Do the 'Fish,' " she says.

People are as loud and lively now as they were three hours ago. Maybe more so. In every direction you turn, people are hanging out. I notice that the branches of the peach trees are sagging, but I don't think much about it. What I do start to think is that maybe Mama will let us keep the piano. She's having such a great time, and she has to see how much Matty loves that baby grand. If the piano stays, he can give concerts like this every night, and I can practice my lessons every day. Surely Mama will want that.

Keep the baby grand. Why not? Today, anything and everything is possible.

Then I spot Daddy.

He slams out of the back door, pointing his fingers at the peach trees. I can't make out what he's saying, but I know he's shouting. He stomps across the lawn and begins to grab legs and arms and pull people down. I think I hear some startled screams, but by the time the two trees are free of people, it's clear no one's hurt. The tree people vacate the premises quickly, leaving puddles of fallen, unripe peaches on the ground.

Daddy jerks his head around, looking everywhere, seeing everything, but not seeming to recognize anyone. I run toward him, but he beats me to the garage and is inside before I get to him. I stand there for a minute. Maybe, I think, nothing will happen. The music continues, the laughs and shouts and singing. Then, abruptly, it all comes to a crashing end.

Gingerly, I step inside the garage.

Daddy is waving his arms about madly, shouting, "Get out! Go home! This ain't no nightclub!" Mama is speechless, and Matty stares in disbelief and anger. Gallon looks like he's frozen with his sticks in midair. Eddie's eyes are cast down.

He doesn't have to shout, I think. Nobody's gonna defy him. People move out of the garage and down the alley, into other yards, and generally away from us without so much as a grumble. I rush back to the patio and send the Tippets away, one because I don't want my father hollering at them, and two, because I don't want them to see him this way.

Claude is the last one to leave. "You okay, Annie?" he asks me in his quietest voice.

"I think so. I'll talk to you tomorrow."

"I wanted to ask you . . ."

"Tomorrow, Claude," I insist and shoo him away.

Back in the garage, Daddy has turned his wrath on Mama. "Why you got all these people up in my trees and trampling your gardens? And what's all this noise in the middle of the night, Sara? And this riffraff round my house?" His eyes widen as he looks around the garage, settling on the piano. "And what is *this?*"

"It's a baby grand piano, Daddy," I say after nobody answers his question.

He eyes fix on Matty. "Where did this come from, boy?"

Matty doesn't answer. Mama starts to explain, but Daddy cuts her off by throwing up his hand.

He speaks to Gallon and Eddie, but keeps looking at Matty. "Pack up all your stuff, you two. And go on home." His voice is almost a whisper now, like he's made himself hoarse from all his shouting. "Matthew, inside."

As slowly as candle wax melting, we all move. All except Matty. He remains slumped on the piano bench, his face a mask.

"I said get in here, boy."

"No."

Mama and I gasp. "Say what?" Daddy's voice rises two octaves.

"Slim," Mama says, grabbing hold of Daddy's arm.

Daddy keeps talking to Matty. "If I had thought of saying 'no' when my father told me to do something, I woulda been slapped so hard my grandchildren would feel it. In my time, a son respected his father."

Matty looks up at him then, meeting his eyes. "Well, things ain't like that now. Nowadays people do what they want to do. Me—all I want to do is play jazz, see? I want to be a musician. I don't want to fix other people's toys, or drive rich people around, or see how high I can jump when the white man tells me to—"

He doesn't get to finish, for Daddy has slapped him across the face. We all freeze. My heart thuds against my chest and seems to drop down into my stomach. I'm too shocked to breathe.

Matty is trembling. His voice shakes, but his eyes are steady. "There ain't never been no respect between you and me, has there? Let's face it. You've never been the kind of father a boy would look up to."

Mama steps in between them quick as a blink. "That's not true, Matthew." She takes a deep breath and her eyes are misty. "When you were a little boy, you looked up to him. Yes, you did. You would wait by the doorway for him to come in from work, and you would spring up into his arms like you had coils on your feet." Mama then turns to Daddy. "And Slim, there wasn't a person alive who could tell you your son deserved less than what he wanted in this life. You would sit for hours, just listening to the sound of his voice. But, today, you don't want to listen to anybody." She shakes her head slowly. "I don't know what's happened to either one of you."

Despite Mama's words, Daddy is still brimming with anger. He seems to struggle for words. "He's gone too far this time, Sara. You can't say nothing in defense of him."

"Slim, the piano's going back," Mama tries to explain.

"That ain't the only thing leaving here," Daddy says. Then he and Matty are shouting at each other. In terror I cover my ears and close my eyes. I want to shout over them to stop, but I can't find my voice. Even though my ears are covered, I hear clearly every mean, cruel, hurtful thing they say to each other.

Finally, Daddy's shouting becomes a harsh whisper. "You think you can do better than I have, huh? Is that it? You're a better man than me? Okay, then, you can just go on out there and prove it. See if you can fight like a man. Because fight or die, you are out of here!"

He slams out of the garage.

Mama follows Daddy. I want to say something to Matty, to let him know I'm on his side about the piano, but I can't even look at him. Everything I've heard is just too awful. My head is reeling and my legs feel weak. Somehow I make my way inside and upstairs to my room. But it's a long time before I fall asleep.

Thursday–Saturday, July 17–19

TRANSLUNAR ORBIT

Chapter Seven

Mama gets me up at six-thirty the next morning. "Wake up, Annie. You're going to Grandmother's house today."

"Huh?" I say groggily.

She kisses me quickly, then flings the covers back. "I couldn't get a baby-sitter. So, come on, now. We can't be late."

It makes no sense to me that I need a baby-sitter today, because Matty doesn't work on Wednesdays or Thursdays, until I remember the night before. My stomach lurches with the memory, and I know a second later, without being told, that Matty's gone.

I rush out of bed to his room. The door is closed, so I put my ear to it. I hear nothing. "Matty," I say softly, praying to hear his answering grunt. Nothing.

I push the door open. His bed, unmade as usual, still looks as if it hasn't been slept in. His dresser drawers, even though they're closed, look empty. His pile of jazz magazines is gone and so are his composition books.

"Matty!" I yelp.

I hurry and wash, get dressed, and race downstairs, hoping he's already up, in the kitchen, crunching on dry corn flakes like he's been known to do. I pass right by the TV, not even stopping to check on the progress of the astronauts. I have to see Matty.

"Good morning, Shoop," Daddy says as I burst into the kitchen. Mama and Daddy are at the table. No Matty.

Mama doesn't look at me when she places a plate in front of me.

Where's Matty? I want to scream, but I'm too afraid to ask. Maybe Daddy's sent him to fight in the Vietnam War. He's threatened to many times. And after Matty said those things to him last night . . .

My heart pounds so hard I think they can hear it too. It's so quiet in the kitchen. The three of us, it seems, are trying not to talk about anything. So I keep the dreaded question to myself.

Twenty minutes later we're on our way to Grandmother's house. It's the worst car ride I've ever had.

The whole way, nobody so much as yawns. The voice from the radio seems to be speaking to empty air:

"On this, the second morning of the lunar voyage of *Apollo 11*, the three astronauts awoke from a restless night to find themselves over 100,000 miles away from Earth. They were awakened by the voice of the flight operations manager."

"This is Houston, Apollo, over."
"Roger, Houston. Good morning (beep)."
"Roger, Commander. Up and at 'em."

The transmission is staticky, with those queer beeps at the ends of sentences like periods. Still, Commander Armstrong sounds alert and ready for his day's mission.

I'm lying down on the backseat so that all I can see out of my window is the unchanging pale blue sky, the tops of trees, and the electrical wires strung overhead. Still, I know exactly when we turn onto Grandmother's street, and just how far down the block we go before we reach her house. When they pull to a stop, I leap up out of the door, with a quick, cold "see ya" to my parents.

Grandmother is waiting on her porch swing. She has on her flowered house dress and the bright pink sweater I'd given her last Christmas. The colors don't match well, but on Grandmother they look like the most welcoming sight.

On the porch I hide behind her short, square frame while she and Mama talk. To avoid having to say another thing to my mother, I quietly slip inside the house.

Granddaddy's already at the dining room table, laying out cards for another game of solitaire. His glasses are halfway down his nose, the brown of the frames matching the deep brown of his skin. Granddaddy's retired, but he still wears his postman's uniform during the day. He looks trim and neat in the pressed outfit, his hair only slightly gray, his eyes golden brown.

"Hi, Granddaddy." He looks up at me, checking to make sure all my parts are okay. "Still wanta be an extranaut?" he says.

"Astronaut, Granddaddy."

"That's what I said, an extranaut." He grins at me over his glasses. I manage a return smile, but I'm not up to his teasing this morning. Grandmother and Mama are still talking outside, so I just sit down beside him and start pointing out plays. He doesn't mind my doing this because he hates to miss a play.

"Granddaddy, why do you play this game so much? Most of the time, Mr. Solitaire wins."

He glances up. "Well, but sometimes I win."

"But not a lot."

He grunts. "Sometimes, though. Lookahere," he says as he collects the lost hand calmly. "Wanta learn another way?"

"Granddaddy, you've already taught me five ways."

"No matter. There're hundreds more. Make you even sharper. Lookahere."

I smile weakly and hold back an impatient sigh. Luckily, though, Grandmother comes in and rescues me. She hugs me with her pink sweater arms. "Did you watch the lift-off?" I ask her quickly.

Grandmother looks at me with alarm. She's like that. She may be old, but she likes to keep up to date with things. Unlike Granddaddy, who's usually sitting somewhere, Grandmother's always moving—planting her many flower beds, or fixing up corsages out of wood fiber in her attic workroom. Rooting through the boxes and boxes of things that she can never throw away, things like egg cartons and milk bottles that she always finds some use for, some use nobody'd ever imagined before. She shakes her head, and the long braid down her back swishes. "No siree, I didn't," Grandmother says.

"Well," I say, "it was really something!"

"Sho nuff?" Grandmother begs me to tell her all about it. I slide away from Granddaddy's cards and lead Grandmother to the living room, filling her in on all the details I can think of. Grandmother likes to hear the technical stuff, even if she doesn't understand it. She asks all kinds of questions, until she's satisfied she's had a good lesson.

"Sho nuff," she says intermittently, when I explain about the amount of fuel the *Saturn V* holds, and the speeds at which the Command-Service Module—the CSM—travels through space. "Right now they're more than 100,000 miles away, in translunar orbit, a little less than halfway to the moon."

"Don't say!" Grandmother exclaims. I keep talking, glad to have someone finally who wants to hear about it. Grandmother doesn't have to rush off to work, or worry about boys who will tease her because she's interested in science. She's the perfect audience for me. "And Sunday night," I say in conclusion, "Neil Armstrong will walk on the moon. Will you watch it, Grandmother?"

"Indeed I will," she responds. "I'ma go mark it right now, so's I won't forget."

She gives me another kiss on the forehead and strides off toward the kitchen.

Maybe it is better that I came here today. Here, nobody will bother me, give me chores to do, or commands to follow. No one will ask me questions about last night or my broken-apart family. I can go to my window box right here in the living room and sit and say nothing all day, if I want to.

In Grandmother's living room are two large windows facing the front yard, on either side of a brick fireplace nobody uses. The windows have a large sill, big enough for me to sit on. I've made a claim on the one nearest the dining room, the one closed in by a wall on one side, the side of the fireplace on the other, and in front, the back of Granddaddy's big leather reclining chair. It's private and cozy, with the sun shining through the yellowed lace curtains hanging in the window.

From my window seat I can watch the street for hours and not a car will come by. Today, I look out and see Grandmother come from around the back, carrying a sack, her gloves, and gardening tools. Grandmother has flowers everywhere, in pots on her two porches, on trellises, around the bases of trees, along the fence, and bordering the porch steps. She even has a garden in her backyard where she grows real food like collard greens and snap beans and cucumbers.

I watch her as she stops at a patch of flowers and bends down, pulling on her gloves. She kneels and places all but one tool beside her. Her back is to me, the pink sweater spread across it. I can't see what she's doing, but I can tell her movements are small and precise, like a watch's. After a while she stands and scoots a foot down the row, then kneels and starts again.

The faint slap, slap of cards on the table reaches me from the dining room.

Nothing changes here. The grass looks the way it always does, like it never grows or needs to be cut. Like it stays green all year, even under the snow. The flower gardens Grandmother has planted around her yard bloom forever. My grandparents seem to me to be the same age now as they were when I first saw them as a baby, as a little girl. I'm older, so they must be also—yet they look the same. The house is the same, the furniture, the sounds, the smells. But everywhere else things have to change. Why? I wonder. Why did Matty have to bring that piano into the house? And why did he have to leave?

Suddenly Granddaddy is standing over me. I see him through a haze of tears. "Annie," he says, his voice strained. "What's wrong, baby girl?"

I can't answer, can only cry louder and harder. Soon, I'm hiccuping and panicking, afraid I can't catch my breath.

"Irena! Irena, come in here!" Granddaddy's pounding against the window, trying to get Grandmother's attention. "This child's crying, Irena!" He looks panicked now too.

Grandmother notices our distress through the window and is by my side in an instant. She touches my forehead, her palm smelling like blossoms. Then I bury my face in her sun-warmed sweater. "It'll be all right, child."

I hate to cry. It's so babyish. Plus, it makes my eyes red and puffy for hours afterward. But now that Grandmother's here, I just want to cry and cry until I'm all cried out. "Matty's gone!" I wail, saying out loud what I've been screaming inside all morning. "And the piano is going— Everything's different—"

Grandmother leads me to her spare bedroom and places me under the white bedspread and sheet. "Get her some water, please, Matthew," she tells Granddaddy. "And an aspirin pill."

He looks only too relieved to be useful—and to get out of there. "I heard her sniffling," he mutters as an explanation. "But I didn't know—"

Something inside me wants to smile at his helplessness, but I'm too busy falling to pieces. And now Grandmother wants to make me take aspirin! "No, Grandmother, please. I hate taking pills." The truth is, I can't take them without the bitter, sticky stone getting stuck in my throat so that I gag and sputter water everywhere. It's scary. And embarrassing.

"You sat up in that window and soaked up a fever. You need to rest now."

Granddaddy comes back with the water and the aspirin. Just the sight of it makes my stomach flip and brings a sour taste to my mouth.

"I don't want to go back home," I say. "Please don't make me. I wanna stay here with you." I mean it too. Grandmother and Granddaddy look at each other, then he nods and leaves. Grandmother sits me up, saying nothing, and wipes my face with a hand-kerchief she's produced from somewhere. Her eyes, bright and clear, understanding but strong, watch me. I try to sniff myself back into composure.

"Please," I plead, my voice a whisper. I want to explain to her why. How the grass stays green here and the flowers bloom big. But what comes out is not that at all. "Mama and Daddy fuss at each other all the time. And now they hate Matty, and they're send-ing the baby grand back. Matty's gone. He's probably gonna get killed over there in that war. And I didn't even say good-bye." I sob and keep going with all the worst things I can think to be sad about. "Maybe they don't like me anymore either. I eat sugar sand-wiches and don't play the piano well and—uh, uh, uh," I run out of breath and start hiccuping again.

"Looka here, Sugar. Ain't no need for you to concern yourself about all that. You just a baby."

"But—"

"Hush, now. Matty'll be all right. He ain't gone to no war."

I blink at her, those words hitting me like a cold, fresh, comforting breeze. Grandmother nods at me. "Just took off last night, on his own, vowing to show your daddy and mama just how talented he is. Said he'll be a 'professional' musician, a star, they'll see. We'll all see, is what he said, then packed his bags and left."

Grandmother shakes her head. "That boy is right and he's wrong."

I sit up. "What do you mean?"

"There's a way to do things and a way not to, Annie. Matty had no business buying that piano without he told somebody. No, sir."

I don't want to interrupt Grandmother, but I feel I have to. She hasn't seen it. She hasn't heard him playing it. "But, it's so beautiful—"

"Sho it is. All God's creations is beautiful. A wonder to behold. But your mama and daddy know y'all can't afford such a thing right now. And Matty shoulda knowed that too. Things take time, and there's a right time for everything."

I can't argue with that, so I keep quiet while she goes on.

83

"Took that piano to make everybody see it was Matty's time to go. All children got to leave home if they want to do something with their life. That's a fact. I did it." She nods. "Sho nuff. It's how I ended up here with all the blessings I got, 'steada staying down South where there wasn't nothing for me. Looka here—I got my own house and a husband who worked a steady job for the whole time we been up here. That's an accomplishment for a colored man."

"Black, Grandmother."

She smiles. "Yes, child—black. Anyway, your daddy and mama—look at all they been able to get for you two. Things we never could for them. 'Cause they stepped out and got themselves skills and education." She nods her head again in that sure way she has. "I'm sorry there were words passed between your daddy and Matthew. But the truth is, it was Matty's time to go. And one day, sho nuff, Annie, it'll be yours."

"Me?" I gasp.

"Sho. How you gonna get to the moon if you never leave home?"

Grandmother laughs as my eyes widen. Her words thrill me and scare me all at once. Of course she's right, but I'd never thought of it that way before. Leave home? Leave my box at Grandmother's window? Leave my street where I know everyone who lives in every house? Leave Earth?

I remember the lift-off from yesterday and how it happened just as Matty's piano was arriving. Matty didn't care about the lift-off, but that's because he was blasting off his own rockets, as he said. I see it now. Just like the astronauts went barreling off toward the moon, Matty was taking off on his own mission. It was time for his launch and he made it.

But what about me? I wonder. When the time comes for me to take off, defy gravity and anything else that's around to keep me on the ground, will I have enough fuel to boost myself up and out and away? Or will I never get off the launchpad, always doomed to sit around and watch other people taking off? Always runner-up. Hesitating, like I did yesterday at the Humpbacked Man's house, so that Claude was the hero, not me. Like I did last night, leaving Matty sitting in the garage without saying one word to him.

"Ooooo," I swoon, falling back on the bed.

"Annie," Grandmother says. "Don't you worry yourself about adult matters. One day, your father and Matthew will work this out. In the meantime," she says and opens her hand, "take this." When I shake my head and let my eyes go wild, she says, "Just put the pill in your mouth, right on your tongue, and drink the water. Just swallow. Relax and swallow."

Reluctantly I put the pill in my mouth, then hurry and take some water so the thing won't start disintegrating on my tongue.

"Now, tilt your head back, Annie, and the pill will just float in that direction. Then, relax and swallow."

I close my eyes and try to do it, knowing I have seconds before the aspirin taste starts to drip down my throat. At the same time that I let out a deep breath, I tilt my head back and swallow. After a few seconds I open my eyes. "It worked! I didn't even feel it."

Grandmother tucks the covers around me and stands up. "Rest now, sugar. Later on we'll have some of that lemon pound cake I baked up. Umm mmm." She stands up. "Everything'll be fine."

I wasn't so sure about that. "But what if . . ." I want to say. What if they don't make up and Matty never comes home? What if that piano goes back and we never can afford another one like it? What if my time comes and I'm really too scared to leave Earth?

Grandmother goes out, humming, "With God, All Things Are Possible." I hate to tell her, but for the first time in my life, I don't know if I believe it.

By the time Daddy and Mama come to pick me up, I'm a limp rag. I have only enough energy to do exactly as I'm told and be civil.

To my surprise, Mama and Daddy look almost happy. No, they *are* happy, laughing with Grandmother and Miss Clara, Grandmother's next-door neighbor. I like Miss Clara, she's funny, but I don't join in on the fun. I'm not angry with my parents anymore. They only did what they had to do, Grandmother said. But how can they be so happy about it?

Daddy tells everybody this great story about how he'd talked to Mr. Shaw at the piano store. "Set him straight, right to his face," Daddy boasts. "He had no business selling to a young boy anyway, without notifying his parents. What kind of businessman takes a kid's word about a major purchase like that?"

Daddy's eyes widen as he looks around at all of us sitting on the porch. "Besides, the boy hadn't signed nothing. So—Shaw's sending somebody to pick it up. Saturday. No charge to us." He smiles triumphantly, like a knight who's just slayed a dragon.

Mama wipes her brow exaggeratedly. "I don't know what got into Matthew."

"Well," Daddy says, rubbing his hands together to finish off the whole matter. "That's the end of that. Now, let's not talk about my foolish son anymore. Makes me mad just to hear his name."

Granddaddy grunts. "Kids today and their ideas. Ain't that right, extranaut?"

I smile and keep quiet.

Once home, I plead exhaustion and go straight to bed. They don't even question me. Strange.

I sleep for a while, but at midnight I wake up and go kneel at my bedroom window. My room faces our front yard, the street, and the houses on the other side. The Tippets' house is right across from ours. I like to get up sometimes, after everyone else is asleep, when it's quiet because only nature, and not people, are making noise. Like the crickets chirping out the temperature, and Mr. Washington's dog going *rou! rou! rou!* at some crawling intruder. Some nights I pretend I'm the ruler of all I can see. But tonight that just seems childish and silly.

It's cooler tonight, I realize, shivering. The crickets are chirping more slowly, a sure sign the temperature has dropped. What if Dodie's right and the rocket going into space has changed the weather? Changed more than that, maybe.

How far from Earth have the astronauts gone? How fast are they falling, falling away from home? Are they asleep now, or wide awake like I am, their hearts racing like mine is now?

I let out a huge, body-shaking sigh.

Saturday the piano goes back. The thought moves across my mind. *Matty is gone* floats behind. *Annie is a coward* flashes and is gone, like a bolt of lightning. I hear Heath's mean laugh like thunder still far away: "Who ever heard of a girl astronaut . . ."

I shiver again and shift my weight around, but I can't get comfortable. Maybe it's because I'm feeling more confused than ever. I know we can't keep the piano, and I think I know why. But I don't know *why* why. And what's worse, I don't know what to do about any of it.

Restless, I crawl back to my bed and sink into the pillows. The words "I wish" start from my mouth, but I stop, scolding myself silently: *Oh, what good does wishing do?*

Chapter Eight

Claude's sharp whistle wakes me up the next morning. On the third one I lift my window and whistle back.

"Hey, Annie," he calls from my front yard. "You still asleep?"

"Well, obviously not, Claude," I snap. He squints up at me, one hand shielding his eyes from the sun.

"I wanta know can I borrow your dad's lawn mower. Just for a couple of hours. Ours is manual and that old man's yard is big." He fidgets, planting one toe on top of the other. Looking at him down there, I get an idea.

"Wait for me!" I yell. Before he can say anything

else, I zip away from the window, wash, and get dressed.

I take my time picking out my clothes for the day and finally settle on my navy-blue pedal pushers and a matching T-shirt. I slip on my whitest socks and carefully fold them down once over my ankles. With my washcloth from the bathroom I wipe old dust from my navy gym shoes and put them on. Then, turning to my mirror, I push all of my hair up into one massive ponytail, braid it, and pin it down. I salute myself in the mirror.

Tumbling down the steps, I'm almost out the door when I hear, "Hold it!" behind me.

"Lindy," I moan. "What are you doing here?"

She's stretched out on the sofa, wearing her usual short pleated skirt and shell top, with two pairs of sweat socks pushed down low on her legs. All Lindy's clothes look like cheerleaders' outfits. "Baby-sitting you, little cousin," she says, flipping her ponytail at me.

"Aunt Sara said to make sure you eat breakfast before you leave out of here," she drawls.

I make a face at her, run into the kitchen, grab an orange, and run back past her. Then, remembering Claude, I go back to the kitchen and grab another orange.

"You look halfway decent today," Lindy calls out.
"You've finally learned how to match your colors. Hah
hah!" Then, "Hey, where are you going?"

I whisk past her. "I'm on a mission," I reply and
slam out the door before she can ask any more questions.

Claude catches his orange with his left hand and
grins at me. We race to see who can peel the orange
the fastest. I have longer nails, so I beat Claude.
Today is starting out well, I think.

The oranges are sweet and juicy, so we manage to
get juice all over our fingers. We rinse our hands off
with the water from the hose and dry them on our
shorts.

"Claude, I want to go with you to the Humpbacked
Man's house. I'll help you cut the lawn."

He looks at me skeptically.

"It's okay," I add quickly. "I don't want any of
your money."

"You don't? Then why are you doing it?"

At first, I hesitate to say anything. What happened
Wednesday night is still unpleasant to think about,
let alone talk about. And how can I admit to Claude
just how much of a coward I had been before, afraid
of the Humpbacked Man?

But then I remember Claude telling me something
once that he'd never admitted to anyone else. How

he sits at his bedroom window late at night too, when everyone is asleep, and pretends he's talking to his father. Pretends his father is still alive. Wishing for things that can't be. Claude may be one person who understands how I'm feeling right now. He might even be able to help me figure out how to get Matty back home.

So, while we take turns pushing the lawn mower all the way to the Humpbacked Man's house, I tell Claude everything. How awful I feel about Matty leaving. How silly I felt the other day, being afraid to face the old man. "So today, I'm going to start by coming face-to-face with the Humpbacked Man. That is the first part of my mission."

"What's the second part?" Claude asks.

I push the mower over a curb. "*That* I haven't figured out yet."

"Did you actually see a hump on his back?"

We're standing in the Humpbacked Man's yard at the top of the hill, his peeling house in front of us. Even under the bright daylight it manages to look sinister.

Claude shrugs casually. "Didn't look all that humped to me, to tell the truth. It's more slumped, than humped." He grins at his cleverness.

"Well," he says, exhaling, "we might as well get

started. But I tell you, Annie, cutting grass is not as easy as you seem to think it is."

He never spoke a truer word. We start mowing in the back, which isn't so bad. But when we move around to the front, we have to deal with the steep hill that is part of the old man's yard. I'm tall for my age, people tell me, and "all skin and muscle," my grandmother says. Well, my muscles get a workout pushing that lawn mower up and down that hill.

After we finish the lawn, we trim the edges along the sidewalk that leads to the front steps. We pull weeds out of the sidewalk cracks and sweep all the stray clippings into the grass. Once we got started on that yard, the whole place began to look much better. By the time we finish, even the house looks welcoming. Well, almost.

Unlike the cool night before, this July day is as hot as ever. Sweat plasters my once crisp T-shirt to my back. Once we try to get a drink of water from the outside faucet, but when we turn it on, the water is all rusty and warm. Then I consider knocking on the side door, the one leading to the kitchen (I know, I peeked), and asking the man for a glass of water. But I don't. It annoys me that I'm still a little leery about facing him. Even if he's not a monster, I still picture him as mean and cranky, with wrinkled hands that could reach out and clutch my throat.

94

Yet, after two and a half hours of hard labor in the hot sun, I don't care anymore what he looks like. Eagerly I follow Claude up to the front door. "I'm gonna ask for a drink," I tell Claude.

"Sure," he says. "Why not?" He knocks on the door.

After a few moments we hear slow, creaky steps across a room. I hold my breath until he appears, shadowlike, behind the mesh screen. The only clear thing I can see is his stringy white hair.

He steps outside, wearing brown suit pants and tan suspenders over a faded white shirt. He is taller than I expected, and skinny. His face is wrinkled, but the skin is clear as a baby's. No, he doesn't have a hump, but yes, he is stooped over like a man who one day leaned over to pick something up and got stuck three-fourths of the way back up. Even so, as he steps past us and surveys our work in his yard, his back seems to straighten a little. When he turns to face us, I look into his clear, copper-colored eyes.

"You children did a good job," he says. His voice seems rusty from not using it enough, like the faucet. He turns to me. "I don't think I've met your helper, Claude."

"That's Annie," Claude says. "And Annie, this is, uh—"

"Otis Blackstone," the man says. He holds out a hand.

I cannot speak for a moment. I think I won't be able to move. Miraculously, though, I lift my hand up to meet his pale, bony one. It is wrinkled, and spotted, but so smooth that when I touch it, I almost draw back.

"Hello, sir," I say.

Before I can utter another word, he says to us, "How about something cold to drink?" The surprise on our faces makes him laugh. "Amanda has some lemonade in the icebox," he says. "Just a little left. She makes it for me but she drinks it herself. Fine with me, though. She makes it too sweet." He motions us inside.

I look at Claude and he whispers, "It's okay." Then he asks, "Who's Amanda?" as he follows Mr. Blackstone inside.

"Amanda? That's my niece. She comes over regularly to take care of her eighty-two-year-old uncle. I let her think she's taking care of me, anyway." He winks at us.

"You're eighty-two!" Claude exclaims. I punch his side and frown at him, but he keeps on. "That means you were born in the last century. I've never met anybody that old before."

Mr. Blackstone doesn't seem to mind. "Born in

96

1886," he says and invites us to sit down as he continues into the kitchen. "Hard to believe it, but it's true," he adds.

"Wow!" I say when he's out of earshot. "Look at this place."

Claude and I gape at each other. We're in this huge living room that must take up one whole side of the house. It's dim because heavy draperies hang over the ceiling-to-floor windows, only slightly parted. All of the furniture is big and wooden, dark and antique-looking. A stiff sofa sits against the farthest wall, in between two of those tall windows. In front of the sofa is a massive coffee table that looks like it took a whole tree trunk to make. I count six matching high-backed chairs with embroidered cushions. They look uncomfortable. Everything, in fact, looks heavy and old, but in good shape. Even the tassled rugs on the floor, though faded, are intact. "Wow," I say again.

"It looks like a museum," Claude adds.

Too afraid to touch anything or move, we just gaze slowly from one side of the room to the other. At the farthest end to our left is a fireplace big enough to step into. Over it sits a marble mantle, bordered in gold, and a gold-leaf mirror hangs above it. I follow along a wall filled with portraits of people dressed in old-fashioned clothes until my eyes reach the opposite side of the room. Then I look down. Then I see it.

It's much bigger than Matty's. And it's a dark mahogany wood instead of black. The gold wheels are dull, not gleaming like Matty's. But the surface of this grand piano is as dust-free as the one sitting in my garage. I know because I go over to the piano and run my fingers across the case.

"It's a baby grand piano," I gasp, proud that I now know to call it by name. "Or maybe it's an adult grand. It's bigger than ours." I start to lift the cover.

"Actually, it's a concert grand."

I jump. The old man is back, holding (a little shakily) two filled glasses. I realize I had forgotten my manners, had just invited myself over to touch his piano. I swallow hard. "Sir?"

"Much larger than the so-called baby grand. The largest one made, actually. This one was made in Germany over forty years ago. It belonged to my wife."

Something about the way he says that last thing makes me look up at him and forget my fear. He is staring at the framed portrait of a lady hanging over a wall near the piano. The lady has a smooth face, deep chocolate in color, and small, dark eyes. She is wearing an old-timey dress and a tight lace collar. Her long fingers are folded quietly together on her lap. "That's your wife?" I say tentatively. Mr. Blackstone nods.

"But she's black." Claude rudely says exactly what I'm thinking.

"Well," Mr. Blackstone says, "so am I."

Claude and I can't help it. We start giggling. To our surprise, Mr. Blackstone laughs a little too. Later, while Claude and I drink the very bitter lemonade Amanda made, Mr. Blackstone explains to us that his great-grandfather was a white man who lived in Georgia, and that's why he's so pale. He points to a picture of his mother, who is as light as he is, and his father, who is very dark. We all end up looking back at his wife's picture again, and nobody's laughing anymore.

"Annie has a grand piano too," Claude says, I think to distract Mr. Blackstone from the sad spell the picture seems to cast on him.

"Do you now, Annie?"

"It's going back to the store," I tell him, and then I have to explain everything. About Matty buying the baby grand. About it being sent back to Shaw's store. Even about Matty's disappearance in the middle of the night. "Boy, if Matty saw your piano, he'd just flip."

"My wife had this specially made. She was a concert pianist. Trained at Juilliard because her parents had money and gave her everything she wanted. She was a spoiled one, that Lizette. Always wanted the best."

He straightens up a little more as he talks about his wife. I quit noticing his back; I'm so interested in his story.

"Lizette, that was my wife, was always pretty and pampered. Only child." Mr. Blackstone nods. "She always had her way. So, when she said she wanted to marry me, that's what happened." He winks at us. "She wasn't an ordinary wife, though. Kept on playing concerts—Paris, London. Even gave some here, right here in this parlor, for the local hoity-toity. You children don't know, but time was this place, Oakwood, was the home of some of Ohio's best families. Colored folks with money."

I start to correct him and say, "Black," but I hold my tongue. The word "parlor" sticks in my mind.

"I never had much affection for those society folks she invited here, but I loved to hear her play . . ."

Claude and I keep silent, waiting for him to finish the story. I already know it's going to be sad.

"Haven't heard that piano played since she died. It's been fifteen years."

I gasp. "You mean nobody plays this piano now?"

"Well, the piano tuner comes once a year. I know it's foolish to spend the money to keep it up. But I do it anyway. Lizette would have wanted me to take care of it." He's almost whispering by now. Abruptly, he turns and counts out five dollar bills. He hands them to Claude. Then he sends us on our way.

We thank him and push our lawn mower back down the hill, not talking much. But we aren't halfway down the block when I stop in my tracks. "Claude," I announce, "I'm going back." I reel around and start back up the hill.

"What for, Annie?" Claude calls.

"I'll tell you later. Rendezvous at The Jungle in one hour. Get everyone together."

"Are you sure?" he says.

"Very sure," I tell him and then break into a run back to the Humpbacked Man's, I mean Mr. Blackstone's, house.

Chapter Nine

I'm on a mission. I finally realize what it is I have to do. And it's going to start at Mr. Blackstone's house.

He is surprised to see me back at his door, but he lets me in without hesitation. I like him already. He's not the least bit mean or cranky, not like you'd expect someone who hasn't had many visitors in fifteen years to be. He offers me more lemonade, and I politely refuse. I don't know how Mr. Blackstone likes it, but Amanda's lemonade could be a lot sweeter.

We sit on his long parlor sofa. "This is the perfect place," I say. Then, I tell him about the plan that came to me: a neighborhood talent show with a special guest, my brother, playing piano. He listens quietly, but when I finish, he still looks skeptical.

"Your parlor is so huge, and you have the piano." I add slowly, "I didn't know your wife, Mr. Blackstone, but I think she would like the idea. She wouldn't want that piano to be silent—forever. And she'd just love Matty's playing. Everybody who hears him does."

And that's just it. I realized so many things as Claude and I were walking home. One thing I realized was that it has been a long time since my father has actually heard Matty play. "If Daddy would only listen to him, he'd have to admit that Matty is talented. He'd have to realize how much having a grand piano means to Matty. He'd have to understand how much Matty wants to play jazz. Daddy was too angry to listen to him the other night. But if I can get him here and let Matty play your concert grand piano . . ."

I've run out of words, so I sit there quietly watching him. Mr. Blackstone clears his throat, stands up, and with his slow walk goes and faces his wife's picture. I'm tempted to add, "Please, please, pleeaase," but that is just not appropriate in this situation, I realize. Minutes pass, but he finally turns around and looks at me. "Okay, Annie. Let's do it."

"Yippee!" I yell, then apologize for yelling in the house.

"You won't have to do a thing, Mr. Blackstone," I explain as I scramble toward the door. "I'll handle all the details."

"Oh, but I must contribute something. I'll have Amanda make up a batch of lemonade."

My cheeks pucker at the thought. I thank him anyway, and we shake hands on the porch. I skip down the steps and out the gate.

Convincing Mr. Blackstone to hold a talent show in his parlor—sort of like his wife had years before, like Mama's aunt Bettye used to do—was easy compared to convincing my parents to come to it will be. Or convincing Matty to be there. After all, I couldn't get Mama and Daddy to watch a lift-off that billions of people across the world just had to see. And I can't even find Matty.

I call Gallon as soon as I get home. "Has he called you? Did he tell you where he is?"

"I tell you, Birdlegs. I haven't seen hide nor hair of him since, well, since the other night when your dad went off."

"Maybe he's with Eddie. Will you call him there?"

"Sure. I'll call around."

"Tell him," I say, "tell him I found another grand piano. Tell him he's got to come play it this Sunday night." I explain to him about Mr. Blackstone and the talent show.

"Get back witcha," Gallon assures me and we hang up.

"Now," I say, dusting my hands. "On to The Jungle."

I'm already there when the Tippets show up. Heath says, "What's up, Annie?" and I can tell by his tone that he's gonna be trouble. "You got another one of your bright ideas?"

"As a matter of fact, I do. It's a very bright idea. I want to have a talent show. We'll invite all the neighbors to come. And we can all perform, and anyone else around here who has talent. There'll be a special guest appearance that I'm keeping secret," (because I can't say for sure our guest will show up) "and we'll have it Sunday in the parlor of Mr. Blackstone's house."

Heath rolls his eyes up. Claude whistles. Sue, Dodie, and Cheron don't understand at all. So, I sit them all down and explain it from the beginning. I tell them about Claude and my visit with the old man. I describe the great parlor room with the museum furniture, the picture of Mrs. Blackstone hanging on the wall, and the concert grand piano. Dodie and

Cheron want to rush over and see it right away.

"No," I say. "We have work to do between now and Sunday. Sue and I will write out the invitations. Claude and Heath can take them door-to-door. Take Cheron and Dodie with you. You can split up and cover more area."

"Wait a minute, wait a minute," Heath butts in. "Who died and put you in charge, Annie? You don't tell me what to do."

Everyone is quiet, looking from Heath to me. I take a long, slow breath. Any other time, I'm ready to fight Heath over who's in charge, or I'm ready to just capitulate and let him be the leader. But not this time.

I turn and face him square. "Every mission has a commander, Heath. I'm the commander of this mission. If you don't want to be a part of it, then don't. We'll do it without you. Of course, I wouldn't think of having the First Official Oakwood Community Talent Show without the Oakwood Black Berets. And since you're the leader of the Black Berets, it makes sense you'd want to be in the show."

I let that sink in. His glare softens to a glower. The Black Berets are a boys' drill team, and Heath is their captain. Claude's in it too. "We'll put you on first, right out front. Everybody will see you before they see anyone else. You can start off doing the Fast Stomp routine, and—"

"You don't have to tell me," Heath interrupts. Then he pauses and looks at me. "I know what routine we'll do first." I nod to him and continue.

"Fine. Then let's do it. The First Official Oakwood Community Talent Show is going to be a blast!"

By the end of the day, when we meet again after dinner, we have twenty neighbors who say they might come, and eleven who say they will. Also, we have all kinds of donations: four dollars and seventy-five cents, five packages of Kool-Aid, a five-pound bag of sugar, and a box of Lorna Doone cookies. "We'll use this for Amanda's lemonade," I say, pointing to the sugar.

It's dark now, so we break up our meeting. We're all supposed to be close to home after sundown. The truth is, tonight I am exhausted and ready for a good night's sleep.

Claude walks me to my front steps and motions me to sit down. I'm finding it hard to keep my eyes open, but we sit there for a while, looking up into the sky.

"Just think," I say sleepily, "in two days there's going to be people walking around up there."

"Yeah," Claude breathes out.

"On the moon—"

"Annie," Claude suddenly says. He puts his hands into the pockets of his overalls and pulls out several little plastic boxes. "Here." He thrusts one into my hand.

It is a ring box. The birthstone ring. Then he hands me the other boxes and starts reaching in his pockets for more. In all, he gives me ten boxes and waits with this little smile on his face for me to open them all. Each time I open another one, I get shorter of breath.

"You like them, Annie? I bought them with the money from the work today. I still owe your dad for the gas. But I can make the money cutting other people's grass. Do you like them?"

"They're beautiful, Claude. But what does this mean?"

He stops smiling. "Mean?"

'Yes," I explain. "Does this mean you want to get married or something? I hope you don't think like Heath that the closest I'll ever get to an astronaut is to marry you!"

Claude breaks up laughing. I watch him for a bit, a little angry, but then I start giggling.

"Come on, Annie," Claude says, trying to catch his breath. "You know I don't think that." He looks me straight in the eyes. "I do like you, though."

Try as much as I can to stop it, a big grin spreads

through my whole body and comes out on my face. I pick up the ten little boxes and stand up to go inside. Claude stands up also. "I do too," I say and run into the house. From the door, I watch him walk tiptoey across the street and into his house.

Saturday morning is soon enough to approach my parents about the talent show. Daddy has come in from mowing the lawn and weeding Mama's rock garden. Working outside always puts him in a cheery mood. Mama has put away the breakfast dishes and is in that limbo state we hardly ever find her in, a time when she has nothing to do and nowhere to be. I join them both in the kitchen.

"Guess what?" I say.

They exchange what-is-she-up-to-now looks.

I continue, trying to sound nonchalant. "We're having a talent show. There's this man who lives in that house on the hill. He's real old, but he's real nice. His name is Mr. Blackstone, and Claude and I took the lawn mower and cut his grass yesterday. Oops!" I grin at Daddy.

"I thought I had more gas in that mower," he complains.

"Claude said he'll pay for the gas. And anyway, I'm going to be the MC for the show, and it's tomorrow. We went from door-to-door, inviting everybody. A lot of them said they'll come. And some gave us money—"

Now it's Mama's turn to interrupt. "You mean you've been going door-to-door begging for money."

I realize I'm losing them in the details. They look like they don't believe one-third of what I've just said. "We're serving refreshments," I add, letting my voice go up like we're serving gourmet dinners. "So will you come?"

"Slow down," Mama says. "And explain this to me again." So I do. Leaving out the Matty part. And to my great relief, they agree to come.

"Yippee!" I shout for the third time in four days. "You have just made me the happiest daughter in the world!" I hug them both and head out of the door.

I walk around the corner to Gallon's house. He comes outside and sits down beside me on his porch. "No luck, Annie. Sorry."

I'm almost speechless. "But what about Eddie Sands? Did you ask him?"

Gallon hesitates too long and I know bad news is coming. "Eddie says Matty called him from the store early Thursday. Said he's gonna quit his job and split. Going to the Big Apple, Annie."

"What?" I gasp.

"New York City," Gallon says, emphasizing every word. "To play jazz."

"That can't be true. Matty wouldn't just leave like that." My heart thuds and becomes a big blob in my stomach. We can still have a talent show, even without Matty, I know, but what's the point? It'd be like taking off to land on the moon but ending up only circling it.

"No," I say to Gallon. "Matty's not gone. He'd have to come say good-bye to me. He wouldn't just leave."

Gallon sighs. "I'll keep looking. You hang in there, Bird."

"He's still here," I tell him. "You'll find him." All the way back home, I cross all my fingers, my arms, and my toes.

Right before the sky in the west turns rosy, I see the Rybickis' moving truck turn onto our street and pull up to our house. It takes me by surprise, because I'd forgotten about the piano going back to Mr. Shaw's store. Mr. Rybicki, Sr., climbs out of the truck on the driver's side, and his son gets out from the other. They walk to the garage. Minutes later, they wheel the wrapped-up baby grand down the driveway, up their ramp, and into the back of the truck.

I cover my ears so I won't hear the clatter of the wheels as they scrape along the concrete and up the metal ramp. It's like I'm watching a silent picture of Wednesday's events, but in reverse. I stare out my window as the truck gets smaller and smaller and finally disappears around the corner.

Of course I feel awful, but I'm finished with crying about it all. Matty will show up. And Daddy will hear him play, and he'll stop talking about sending Matty to war. Matty will come back home and play Mr. Blackstone's piano whenever he wants to. My family will be together again, and everyone will be happy. And tomorrow, men will walk on the moon.

Sunday, July 20, 1969

LUNAR LANDING

Chapter Ten

Even though I remind Mama that today, for the first time *ever*, men will walk on the moon, and even though I remind her that in less than ten hours I will be standing in front of all our neighbors and emceeing the talent show, she still makes me get up and go to church.

As she's fastening my two braids to my head with heavy barrettes, Mama starts humming "Motherless Child." I catch her eyes in the mirror, but we don't say anything about it. Nobody has mentioned Matty's name since Thursday.

"There," she says and pats my shoulders.

I hate this style. My braids are too tight, and the barrettes feel like handcuffs for my hair, pulling the two braids even tighter. "Yes, ma'am," I manage to say.

"Come on down and eat," Mama says, collecting her brush and comb to leave.

"Mama?" I say. She stops and turns around. She has on her sky-blue dress suit and matching shoes. Her sandy-red hair is curled all over and soft. "You look pretty today," I tell her. Then I say, "Mama?" again, and this time I just blurt the rest out. "Don't you even miss Matty?"

She stops at the door for a long minute, then turns around and looks me straight in the eye. "No, I do," Mama says and walks out chuckling.

I get a big surprise when I go downstairs to breakfast. Daddy is seated at the table, dressed in his navy pinstriped suit. "You're going to church?" I exclaim.

"That's right, Shoop." It's been ages since my daddy has gone to church. "And then I'm coming home, and we're all gonna sit down and watch the television this afternoon. Gonna watch the men land on the moon." He shakes his head like he can't believe it, but he has to because it's true.

"And then," he adds with a lift of his coffee cup for a toast, "I'm going to take my wife and my suit to the First Official Oakwood Community Talent Show, hosted by that toast of the town, Miss Annie Armstrong! How sweet it is!"

116

Our church has no air conditioning, and Reverend Leander reminds us that contributions to the new building fund will mean we don't have to melt like candles in the sun next summer. I try not to squirm because that only makes you hotter, but my mind won't hold still, so why should my body? Every word Reverend Leander says springs out into a hundred more thoughts in my head. When he mentions something about "shooting those NASA rockets into the heavens," my thoughts fly off so I don't even hear what he's saying about them. When he says something about man being simply a "child in the hands of God," I can't help it. I start thinking about Matty.

He's not coming, I moan to myself one minute. And then I say, *He has to come,* the next minute. I try to concentrate on the sermon, but then I lose myself with these silent prayers I keep sending up to God:

"God, this is Annie. How do you read?"
"Roger, Annie. Reading loud and clear (beep)."
"Roger, God. Let's bring Matty back home."
"You betcha (beep)."

"In just five minutes, the lunar module spacecraft will make contact with the surface of the moon, the first time ever that man will land on another celestial body. No one knows exactly what will happen when the spindly legs of the LM sink down onto the lunar surface. But after eight years and over twenty billion dollars, this is what the *Apollo* project is all about." The TV newsman's face is solemn, but his droopy eyes are lit up.

Mama giggles. "What do you say about that, Slim?"

Daddy rubs his chin. "It's incredible, Sara. You got to admit, it's incredible." He blows out softly.

I'm sitting between them, watching the final stages of the lunar module's lunar descent. Mama and Daddy look like two eager schoolchildren on the first day of school.

"This is so exciting, isn't it, Annie?" Mama says.

I stop myself from reminding her that I said those very same words four days ago, and she just waved me away. "No, it is," I reply, trying to sound as sarcastic as I can.

The newsman's voice is more excited now, and he has taken off his glasses. The lunar landing is only minutes away.

And this is when the phone rings.

Now, mind you, I've been keeping one ear cocked to the telephone all day. Believing, hoping, praying in church, and then hoping again back at home that Matty would call. Not Gallon. Matty. I want to hear his crazy, "Whassis sisappenin'." I want to hear him say he's on his way—back home.

Well now, two minutes before the lunar landing, the phone does ring.

I race to get it first. "Hello," I whisper.

"Annie, is that you?"

Matty. I take a deep breath. "Yep," I say, trying not to draw attention to myself. "Where are you?"

There is some hesitation before he says, "In town. Never made it to New York. Got a gig going on right here in town."

"Really!" I exclaim. Mama glances at me. I make my face blank.

"Gal tells me you got big plans for tonight. What's happening?"

"What he told you," I say secretively.

"Oh, I see. You can't talk. Okay then, I'm just calling to tell you—I'll be there."

"You will? That's good. Very good. Starts at six. Get there early. You know where it is?"

Matty laughs. "The Humpbacked Man's house. Though how you swung that gig, I don't know. You're amazing, Annie. Later, alligator!" He hangs up.

"Who was that?" Mama asks when I return.

"Claude," I tell her.

"Sssh," Daddy hisses. "Y'all listen."

119

So we do. I don't think I take a single breath the next ninety seconds. The surface of the moon looks like leftover cereal in a bowl, gray, with holes in some places, and little lumps in others. I know that those holes are really craters, some of them miles across. And the lumps could be boulders as big as a car. Every second brings Neil Armstrong and Buzz Aldrin 300 feet closer to the moon, and with each passing second, our eyes get wider and wider. Then we hear Neil Armstrong's voice. "Houston, Tranquility Base here. The *Eagle* has landed."

Everyone all over the world exhales at once. The newsman on TV exclaims, "Hot diggity dog!" I think we all agree.

Chapter Eleven

I let Mama help me pick out my dress for the show, even though we both know I can choose for myself now. We agree on the yellow sundress with the ruffled short sleeves and the lace pockets up front. Mama still won't let me wear stockings, so I settle for yellow knee socks. I have already polished my black patent leather shoes and cleaned my white gloves. Mama gives me a small pair of yellow flower earrings to wear and then ties my hair back with a yellow ribbon. After a few moments we both agree the ribbon is too much.

"Okay, Annie, you do your own hair," Mama says and she leaves me before my mirror in my room. I think about it for a second, cocking my head one way and then another, trying to remember styles I've seen on other people and in pictures. I decide to gather it all up into a ponytail at the top, and then fasten it into a French knot with bobby pins.

"You did that?" Mama asks, amazed as she comes back to check on me. She seems to think I have some secret hairdressing genie hidden in my room. I nod at her and turn around so she can inspect the whole look.

"Annie," she says, "that's mighty nice. You are just growing up right before my eyes."

When I get to Mr. Blackstone's house at five-thirty, Heath and Claude are already setting up chairs in the parlor. I tell them "hi," then raise my eyebrows at Mr. Blackstone. He motions into the hallway and points to a closed door. "He's in the study," Mr. B. says.

I knock, then open the door. Matty is standing by another floor-to-ceiling window, in dark sunglasses, looking out into the yard. He's dressed in a suit jacket and jeans, a white shirt and a tie, and he looks like the men on the back covers of Daddy's jazz albums.

I run over to him, and he holds his palms up for a "five." "Whassis sisappenin'?"

"Did you see the piano? Isn't it beautiful?"

Matty shakes his head. "Yeah, Annie. But, tell me, how did you get that old man to let you do this? I mean, nobody even sees him, and you get all of us into his house for a talent show."

"I'll explain all of that later. First, we need to get organized."

Matty salutes me. "Roger, Commander Armstrong. What's the plan?"

"Play 'Motherless Child' first. Like you did the other night. Then some classical music. Everybody'll love that. Then, play your jazz—"

He looks at me for a moment, then walks over to a chair and sits down. "Is Daddy coming?"

I follow him. "Yep."

"Does he know I'm here?"

I swallow. "No. But Matty, if I told him, he might not've come. And if he didn't come, he'd never hear you play. And, if he never hears you play, how will you two ever make up so you can come back home?"

Matty cuts me off. "Annie, a couple of jazz songs are not gonna change his mind."

"Just try it, Matty." I'm clutching his hands.

He pulls away from me, alarmed. "Hey, don't damage the goods here."

"Okay, look. Just play. Play as long as you want. Whatever you want. You can play 'Twinkle, Twinkle, Little Star.' I want Daddy, Mr. Blackstone, everybody to hear you play."

He smiles at me and nods. With my fingers crossed I go back to the parlor to help Heath and Claude set up the chairs.

The First Official Oakwood Community Talent Show starts promptly at six o'clock. Like I'd promised, Heath and the Black Berets perform first, right out front in Mr. Blackstone's yard. Nine of them form three rows, and Heath stands out in front. They have their berets pulled down low over one eye. All of them wear black jeans and white T-shirts. Their heavy shoes echo against the front of the house as they stomp and march back and forth. "To the left, hut! To the right, hut! To the rear, hut! Now freeze! Defrost!" Heath is where he always wants to be, bossing everyone else around.

After the Black Berets finish, to great applause, I usher everyone inside to take seats. More people have come than we expected, so we have to get Mr. Blackstone's kitchen chairs and add them to the folding ones we borrowed from the church. Nobody minds being squeezed in. Granddaddy and Grandmother have a seat on the sofa, with my father and mother. Mr. Blackstone has one of the high-backed chairs. He looks so distinguished in his brown suit, crisp white shirt, and bow tie.

I wait calmly until people are settled in and looking

around expectantly. Then, I step right out onto our "stage," an area of the parlor just inside and to the left of the hall entrance. Surprisingly, I'm not at all nervous. I walk to the center, get into my best spelling-bee posture, and begin.

"Ladies and gentlemen," I say slowly and clearly, as Mama has always instructed me to do, "welcome to our talent show. Before we start, we'd all like to say 'thank you' to Mr. Otis Blackstone." I wait while everyone claps politely, nodding to Mr. Blackstone. "Now, let's begin. The first part of our program is the children's fashion show."

Sue starts the music playing. We had to bring our own record player because Mr. Blackstone never bought one. He doesn't have a television either, and he says he never uses his telephone.

The first to model is Cheron. She is wearing her complete Easter outfit, including the bonnet, gloves, and pocketbook. Five other little girls strut out in playclothes, church clothes, and bathing suits. Sue had shown them how to walk and turn and strike a pose. She even went so far as to put lipstick on them. The audience oohs and aahs and applauds loudly. Cheron, ever the princess, has to be the last one off the stage.

Next is a duet, sung by Dodie and Sue. Believe it or not, Dodie has a good soprano voice. The only time she and Sue can work in harmony is when they sing. They sing every verse of "Swing Low, Sweet Chariot," and they sound really nice.

While they are singing, Claude joins me off to the side. He has removed his black beret. "Did you watch us?"

"Yes," I say with a smile. Then Heath sidles up.

"Where's your special guest, Annie?" he sneers.

I look at him and then turn my attention back to the stage. "Take off your hat in the house, Heath," I say.

The talent show rolls on without a hitch. Wendell Pointer plays his clarinet, a song none of us recognizes. Then Traci and Staci Austin do a dance to Aretha Franklin's "Respect." While they're performing, I slip out to the study. "Matty, you're next." He joins me in the hallway and stands just outside the parlor, out of view. When the Austin twins finish, I go back onstage.

For the first time this evening, I'm nervous. My heart has sped up and my throat feels dry. I'm standing in front of everyone, just looking at them and beyond them. Briefly, I look at Daddy, and then I see Mr. Blackstone make a motion. I look at him and he nods and smiles, then his eyes fix on Lizette Blackstone's picture. Taking a deep breath, planting my feet solidly and folding my hands in front of me, I introduce the last part of the talent show.

"Ladies and gentlemen, we now come to a special part of the show." I walk over to the grand piano and with Claude's help, I lift the cover and prop it open. The neighbors go ooooh and aaah.

"This piano belonged to Mrs. Lizette Blackstone, who was a famous concert pianist. She played all over the world, but her favorite place to play was right here in her parlor. So, she had this concert grand piano made just for her, and she gave concerts right here where we sit today." I pause briefly. "But fifteen years ago she died, and there were no more concerts. No more music played on this piano."

I swallow over the lump that is suddenly in my throat. "Today, this piano will be played again, by someone who loves piano playing as much, I believe, as Mrs. Blackstone did. This person is not famous yet. But one day he will be, I just know it. Ladies and gentlemen, on the piano, my brother—Matthew Sterling Armstrong."

Matty strides in and goes right to the piano bench. He has on those sunglasses still. Without so much as a glance toward the audience, he sits down and kicks off his shoes. A few people clap at first, but then everyone sits silently, watching Matty or glancing at my father. Some of them were there Wednesday night when Daddy went off, and others have heard about it. So everyone is waiting, like me, to see what will happen.

Please don't walk out, Daddy. Please, please, please.

Matty starts to play "Motherless Child," his fingers rolling up and down the keys like water over a fall. He speeds up and slows down, plays a crescendo and then a diminuendo. The strains of that song pour out into the room, and I know it gets to people because I see them holding their hearts and dabbing at their eyes with handkerchiefs. Mama and Grandmother hold hands. Granddaddy is rocking a little. And Daddy—he's just sitting there, blank-faced, not looking at Matty at all.

By the time he finishes his first song, people are no longer afraid to applaud. They cheer and whistle, but Matty just ignores them and starts another song. Each time he finishes, they clap some more, but he keeps on playing. He ends with his song, "The Living Is Easy." When he finally pulls his hands from those piano keys and stands up, people jump out of their seats and are on him in seconds, patting his back, shaking his hands.

Matty tries to look humble, but he can't pull it off. "Thank you. I'll be playing at Gil's, downtown, on weekends. Come and see me."

Mama has made her way through the throng and

is standing proudly beside her son. But Daddy is no longer in the room.

I go out into the hallway, looking for him. He's not there. I look out the front door. He's standing on the sidewalk at the end of Mr. Blackstone's porch.

I whisper his name. I want to go out there with him, he looks so lonely and sad. Why is he sad? Why can't he be proud and pleased like the other people here? Suddenly, I feel like just bawling because it seems like it's all for nothing. There's nothing else I can do. All the planning and convincing others to do things, the running around. The frantic wait for word from Matty. It was all for nothing because Daddy is still mad at my brother. I slump against the door frame and just watch him.

Mama comes out of the parlor and spots me. Matty is close behind her. Together, we all look out at my father alone on the sidewalk. Then Mama opens the door and goes out. We don't say anything, but just follow her.

The sun is disappearing, but it's not dark yet, so no stars are visible and neither is the moon. Still, Daddy keeps his eyes fixed on the sky, or rather, he's looking toward the place where the sky and earth meet, far off in the distance. When we get close to him, he turns and looks at the three of us.

"Tell him, Matty," I urge. "Tell him about the

job here, playing piano." Matty doesn't say a word. "Tell him!"

Matty still won't open his mouth.

"It's true, Slim," Mama offers. "They're paying him. Not much, but it's a start."

After what seems like an eternity, Daddy clears his throat. "A job, huh? Playing piano." He chuckles, but his eyes are not laughing at all. He looks back at the horizon. "That's good, son." His voice cracks. "Really . . . good."

Daddy is shaking his head even as he's saying those words, like he can't believe what he's heard.

"It's true, Daddy," I say. "It really is true."

Daddy looks at me and finally smiles a real smile. "Well, Shoopaloop," he says, "how sweet it is."

We stay out there together a while longer, talking very little, but huddled underneath the darkening sky. Matty fills in some of the details of his "gig."

"Working at Shaw's during the week and playing on weekends, I'll make enough money to support myself. So I got myself a pad, a room, downtown." He looks at me. "You won't have your old brother to kick around the house anymore, Annie," he jokes.

I think about that for a minute. "Well, that's okay," I finally reply.

Eventually we go back inside and join our neighbors around the refreshment table. I take my share of congratulations and pats on the back, and smile and laugh with everyone. But most of the time my mind is thinking about everything that's happened in the last five days, how the excitement has been so mixed up with the sadness. But for all that's happened, I wouldn't have given up those few minutes outside with Mama, Daddy, and my brother for all the cheese in the moon.

Chapter Twelve

Mama lets me stay up as long as I want, in front of the TV, to watch the moon walk. Has this been a miraculous day or what?

I watch the shadowy pictures of Neil Armstrong and Buzz Aldrin as they step off of the lunar module ladder and place their footsteps on the moon. "That's one small step for man," Neil Armstrong reports, "one giant leap for mankind."

He may be a man, but he skips and leaps around on that moon like he's a six-year-old kid.

By 1:00 A.M. I'm ready for bed. I go to my room and sit at the window, peering out onto my sleeping kingdom and the wide black sky above it.

It's funny, looking at the moon now, barely a crescent. From here, it looks like nothing's changed. It's the same glowing white night-light I've seen all my life. And yet, there are men up there, and the footprints they made on the dusty surface will last forever. For them, for the moon, for us, nothing will ever be the same.

I've changed too. I don't look any different, but I'm not the same ten-year-old I was before lift-off Wednesday, before the baby grand appeared, before Matty disappeared, before all that has happened in the last five days. I still have some things to be sad about. Matty's not coming back here to live, for one. Everyone agrees that's the right thing for him to do. But I'll miss him.

Of course, there're a lot more things to be happy about. The First Official Oakwood Community Talent Show was a great success, and that's "no brag, just fact." Plus, Mr. Blackstone says we can visit him any time and explore in his big museum of a house. There's an attic and a basement, and all kinds of fun waiting there, I'm sure. Who wouldn't be happy about that?

And then there's Claude. He's been a good friend to me, I realize. Still, I don't know what to make of him and his ten birthstone rings. What do they mean? I still have not put one single ring on.

Anyway, now I have to sleep. An astronaut has to be rested and well prepared for her next mission. Notice, I said *her* next mission?

About the Author

Joyce Annette Barnes was born in Ohio, the setting for *The Baby Grand, The Moon in July, and Me*. She says, "When I was young, my oldest brother actually did purchase on credit a piano that just showed up at our house one summer day. My parents knew nothing about the purchase, and very soon the piano disappeared again. I was too small to understand what had happened; the novel is just what I've filled in."

Ms. Barnes is an assistant professor of English at Catonsville Community College in Maryland. An award-winning playwright, she first wrote Annie's story as a play called "The Baby Grand" that captured first place in the WMAR-Arena Players Black Playwrights' Contest and was later produced on television. She lives in Frederick, Maryland, with her husband and two children.